I0583925

MING THE MERCILESS

ANOTHER STEAMING PILE OF CRAP FROM

RALPH ROTTEN

<u>Index</u>

This page intentionally left blank,
by order of the great & imperious
Wizard of Oz.

Pay no attention to the man behind the curtain.

The Interview

Running a hand through her mane of golden hair, ace reporter Polly Purehart remained patient as her cameraman finished setting up his gear on one side of the throne room. Although she was doing a good job of appearing nonchalant on the outside, inside she was ready to burst. After years of chasing leads and hard work she was finally about to land the interview of her career. This was it; her big swan song, the piece that would make her a galactic star. In just a few minutes she would be interviewing the biggest despot in the galaxy; Emperor Ming.

The room was imposing; composed of multiple gleaming archways that came together like the spine of a great beast. Beneath her feet, flawless black marble covered the floor in every direction. Allowing her eyes to follow the steps upward, she could see the throne that commanded the center of the room. Tall and imposing, the ornate chair was studded with jewels and gold trim. Raising a single eyebrow, the journalist silently clucked her disapproval over the throne. Hands on hips, she estimated that the damned thing cost more than her whole home.

Glancing up, Dave the cameraman was momentarily distracted as he stared at Polly. She was a stunning creature with her golden hair and sharp curves. During the month that he had worked with her, he had found it extremely difficult to focus with her around. But then again, most men felt that way about Miss Polly Purehart. Intelligent, talented, and gorgeous, it was no wonder she was a favorite all across the galaxy.

Leaning on his tripod, Dave realized he had been ogling the reporter and finally spoke up.

"We're good to go. Sound and video check out, and this room has really great acoustics." Giving a smile, the cameraman did his best to look her in the eye.

Behind them the big doors to the chamber opened; the sound echoing throughout the room. Glancing that way attentively, Dave and Polly could see Emperor Ming's massive entourage. First there was a full platoon of robo-guards, each armed with the very latest in warfare. Then came the Emperor's elite personal guards; all dressed in blood-red armor that made it difficult to tell if they were organic or synthetic. *No one knew what lived under those Duranium-armor suits.*

Following the soldiers was Lotus and his personal entourage of two. Polly had met the greasy-haired *Chief Minion* earlier when they first came aboard the station. He had tried to restrict her to a specific list of questions *(that HE had written)* but she refused. When that had failed, the gangly little man had tried to order her to only ask upbeat questions. But once again she had impolitely refused. Truly, Polly had found Lotus to be nothing more than a worm...*a worm on a leash.* That had been the term that Dave had come up with. Indeed, she found the term fitting for the creepy little man known to be the Emperor's top flunky. She could almost feel his beady little eyes roving her form. *The little pervert never looked her in the eyes.*

Returning her attention to the parade before her, Polly watched another platoon of guards & minions pass through the doorway. Then finally came the main event, as a dozen robo-slaves pushed a massive granite hoverboard. Standing atop the floating platform, in a regal pose, stood the Emperor Ming.

He was quite a lot to take in really. From the gleaming shaven head, to the flowing robes of crimson, he seemed like a splash from a comic book. With sharp eyes fixed on something in the distance, he gave the impression that he was deep in thought as the hoverboard finally came to a stop. Stepping off the platform, he strode confidently up the last few steps before carefully seating himself in the throne.

Another moment passed while Lotus whispered something urgent into the Emperor's ear. Only after the Chief Minion was done did the man in the throne acknowledge Polly and Dave. Remaining impassive, he could not help but stare at Polly. He had seen her on the galactic feed, but seeing her here in person was another thing altogether. Looking her up and down, he understood why so many of the heroes had granted her interviews.

"Emperor Ming." Polly spoke out loudly from the base of the steps. "Or may I call you by your other name: Ming the Merciless?"

Immediately Lotus rushed forward, his greasy hair hanging down in his eyes. "That is absolute heresy! Fake news! I will have you know that the Master has always been extremely humane when he is exterminating a species. You will be flogged for your disloyalty. Guards, bring in the flogger!"

Polly was about to point out the idiocy of that statement when she noticed that Ming had simply waved his hand dismissively. A grimace across his face said that he was not in complete agreement with his chief minion. Rushing back up the steps, Lotus leaned in close as the two exchanged words.

"You don't want me to have her flogged for her insolence?" Lotus seemed surprised.

"No, no. I actually like that moniker. It has real marketability." Speaking in a low voice, Ming rubbed his bearded chin.

"Ming the Merciless?" Puffing up in his suit, Lotus reconsidered the title.

"It has a certain *geneseque* about it. It would make an excellent campaign slogan, don't you think?" Still stroking his beard, Ming relished in the moment.

"B-but sir, we don't have elections..?" Lotus was momentarily unsure.

"Exactly!" Slamming a skinny fist into his palm, Ming emphasized his point. Giving a deep laugh, he was immediately joined by his henchman. Enjoying an evil chuckle together, the two finally returned their attention to the buxom reporter who glared at them.

"And what do you have to say about accusations that you obliterated an occupied star system in the Rigel sector?" Sharp eyes, Polly had no intention of being a fluff reporter. She wanted hard-hitting documentary.

"Pernicious lies!" Slamming down a fist on the arm of his throne, Ming's voice echoed throughout the hall.

"Blevins was an occupied world when you wiped out its star and turned the entire system into a deep-freeze." Standing her ground, Polly had felt a jolt of fear earlier. Although she was a top-rated journalist for the biggest periodical in the galaxy, she had to keep in mind that this was Ming the Merciless. He had people executed on a whim. While she preferred to think that she was too important to be murdered, she knew this to be untrue. The Emperor's list of fallen foes was a long one indeed.

"Pish-posh." Ming dismissed it with the wave of a hand. "That was a perfectly legal action, performed under strict compliance with galactic eminent-domain laws. Those people were notified of eviction well in advance, and provided resources to relocate to one of the nearby star systems. A minor inconvenience for the people of a single star system so that the entire galaxy could enjoy the benefits of a galactic freeway system."

Piping up from behind his boss, Lotus added his own two cents worth.

"And that star was about to destroy itself anyhow. Really, we were doing them a favor." The minion's shrill voice only drew a harsh look from his master. A split second later and Lotus was back cowering behind the throne again.

Polly had just begun to ask her next question when the far wall erupted in an explosive flash. The sound was deafening as bits of debris flew past them. Immediately Dave grabbed his camera and found a corner to hide in. Ming stood defiantly towards the new threat, his jewel-encrusted hands clenched in fists.

Glancing around, Polly pretended to be surprised. In truth she had known all along that this was coming; the top button of her blouse was secretly a stellar beacon. The Captain had assured her that she would have complete plausible deniability, and land a front-page story as well. *She simply had to go with the story.*

Stepping through the dust came a well-built man. Clad in light armor over a bodysuit, he paused long enough for the camera to catch his good side before speaking.

"Ming! I have finally tracked you down to your secret lair." Raising a fist, the champion promised destruction to the man on the throne.

"Captain Legend." Ming's shrill voice seethed as he uttered the words. "I thought I killed you on Tau Seti."

"No, you certainly tried. Left me to be cut in half with a particle beam, but I managed to get free from my restraints, just in the nick of time." Hands on hips, Captain Legend showed his pride at having escaped the clutches of his foe.

"That is a mistake that I can readily correct. Guards; kill this man and bring me his face so that I may wear it to a costume party." Thrusting a bejeweled finger at his foe, Ming commanded the robo-guards to surge forward with murderous intent.

Taking cover behind one of the columns,

Polly could see the robots attack with everything from energy cannons to chainsaws. Using his defensive shield to selectively block the bots, Legend used his super-strength to smash the robots that were foolish enough to get within range of his flaming-sword. One after another the synthetic warriors were torn to pieces as Captain Legend worked his way towards the throne.

Acting aloof, Ming seemed to have no concerns for the speed at which his adversary was advancing through his mechanized horde. Pretending to examine his nails, he slumped on the throne just a short distance from the fray.

Still more robots poured through the main portal and into the chamber. Firing at anything that moved, they attacked the hero *en masse*. The sheer volume of gunfire, rockets, and flechettes being unleashed on the man was amazing. Polly had a hard time believing that anyone, even the legendary Captain Legend himself, could have survived all of that.

But then, before the dust could even clear, as the robo-guards all stood recharging their energy weapons for their next volley, a massive burst of energy emanated from the spot where Legend had last been seen. Like an EMP blast, the bio-energy pulse shut down every robo-guard in the room. Even the Praetorian Guard all fell useless to the ground, their cybernetic implants burnt and fused.

Striding forward purposefully, Captain Legend appeared out of the dust. His suit scuffed and damaged, blood dripping from a few places, the hero had seen better days. Nevertheless, he intended to make Ming pay for his sins.

But he only made it a few paces before he felt the most curious sensation. His legs still moved but he could not feel the ground beneath his feet. Backpedaling, he discovered he was being held aloft by an unseen energy force.

"Oh, did you think it would be that easy to apprehend me, as if I were some common bail-jumper?" Ming emphasized each word of his sentence as he finally stood. With his enemy floating at eye level just a few feet away, he had a captive audience.

"What in the hell is this?" His legs pumping wildly, Captain Legend was angered by this trick.

"Really, Captain Legend. After all these years do you still regard me as a simpleton, incapable of complex thinking?" Leaning forward, Ming was careful to stay out of range of his flaming sword. "I saw right through your plan from the very beginning. Guards: bring me the spy."

As new robots poured into the room, they seemed to ignore Dave and his camera. Instead, most of the robots formed a perimeter around the Captain while three more scooped up Polly. Dumping her at Ming's feet, the robo-guards retreated quickly.

"I knew all along about your little transmitter." Using a sharpened fingernail, the Emperor cut off Polly's top button, exposing her cleavage in the process. Smiling as she tried to close the top of her shirt, Ming spoke his mind. "I can see why the Captain likes you so much, such a delicate little flower, indeed."

Ming made a subtle motion with one hand, and immediately a pair of robo-guards grabbed Polly by the arms and held her. Stepping forward, the Emperor waved a hand to tighten the field restraining the Captain. As the buzzing sound increased, it was obvious that it was causing the hero a significant amount of pain. Laughing aloud, Ming relished not only in Legend's pain, but the expression on Polly's face each time he amplified the restraining field. Clearly it pained her almost as much as it did the Captain each time he tortured the man.

"What are you planning now?" Seemingly resigned, Captain Legend had been led there by a murky set of clues. If he was going to die, he at least wanted to know why.

"Now that my plan to remove you from the chessboard has been accomplished, I will begin construction of the stellar wall in the Nexus region." Shrugging, Ming had been planning this for a very long time.

"But that will destroy seven star systems, three of which are occupied." Shouting out, Polly struggled against the robotic hands that held her.

"They will be duly notified of formal eviction proceedings, the full letter of the law will be followed. Yes, yes, no animals will be harmed in the making of this stellar wall." Frowning, the Emperor dismissed her complaints.

"Whatever you do to me, I ask that you please just let Polly go. Don't hurt her, it was all me. She had no idea I installed the tracker." Showing his first true concern, Captain Legend worried about the collateral damage.

"Don't hurt her? Let her go?" Ming's voice went up an octave as he mocked his adversary. Showing a grin, he moved over to the journalist, close enough to sniff her hair as he hovered over her. "Oh no. Miss Purehart and I will be getting to know each other...*intimately* over the next few months."

Taking a moment to leer over the shapely reporter, Ming finally straightened up and returned his attention to the Legend.

"You, however, will not be riding in first class with us. In exactly nine minutes you will become part of a rapidly expanding ball of energy. Congratulations Captain, you get to be six moles worth of atomic material in the first gate of the Galactic barrier. Not only will you *be* history, but you will be a *part* of history. Isn't that exciting?" Reaching out, he pinched Legend's cheek.

"You mean this was all just a trap?" Shocked, Captain Legend was only now seeing the big picture.

"Ahhhh, now he finally grasps it." Chuckling, Ming only had to glance at Lotus to encourage the minion to join in on the laughter.

"Nooo, let Polly go, and you can do whatever you want to me." Struggling vainly against his invisible restraints, the Captain knew that things looked grim.

"But…I can already do whatever I want to you…and Miss Purehart. Goodbye Captain Legend, you have eight minutes before you become pure, energy-laden, plasma. You have been a worthy adversary, I shall mourn you." Making a droopy face, Ming mocked his foe.

"Really?" Captain Legend was surprised.

"No." Shaking his head, the Emperor simply blinked his eyes before moving off toward the waiting ship. Behind him robo-guards dragged Miss Polly along with them.

Only after the room was empty did Dave the cameraman finally step out of the shadows. Looking left then right, he was clearly terrified at the piles of bodies. Turning the direction that Ming and the others went, he scurried out the door after them. *He certainly did not want to stay on the station.*

Seated in the ship's observatory, Polly

had a good view of the orbital station through the curved window overhead. It was just a dot of reflected sunlight from the nearby star, nothing more. With the count-down timer announcing the time till detonation, Polly squirmed uncomfortably in her chair.

"So that's it? You are going to leave Captain Legend there on the station to die?" Angry, Polly railed against the inevitable.

"Yes, the Thorium reactor directly beneath his feet will implode, creating a gravitational lens along the edge of this star. Unless there is a power failure in the next three minutes, he will be turned into blue plasma." Satisfied with himself, Ming sat up abruptly. "Excuse me, I need to go to the little arch-villain's room. At my age the plumbing is somewhat less predictable than when I was a young henchman."

Excusing himself, he had been gone for more than a minute when Polly could have sworn she saw the tiniest little dot scuttle away from the station. Relieved to see that Captain Legend had managed to escape, she was surprised when the station erupted into a bright ball of energy before shrinking down to a pinpoint of light. The journalist sat stunned from the stellar event she had just witnessed. After the longest moment she finally turned to Dave. Standing in the back of the room, the cameraman had made a point to stay out of the way.

"You got that on film, right?" She asked.

"Oh yeah." Dave confirmed from his spot against the wall. He had found it particularly odd that while the soldier-bots carefully controlled Polly's every movement, they had made no effort to corral the cameraman. The twenty-something photo journalist was left to wander about filming things as he pleased.

"Oh, curses!" Clenching his fist, Ming returned to find that he had missed the event. "Damned synthetic bladders, made me miss the ribbon-cutting ceremony."

"You murdered him!" Pretending she had not just seen the escape pod leave the station, Polly spat out the words. "What now? Is this where you ravage me like you promised Captain Legend you would do?"

"Ravage?" Ming seemed to mull the word over before he realized the source. "Oh, no I meant we would get to know each other intimately because I want you to write my biography."

Polly blinked twice as she tried to understand his angle. "You're not going to rape me?"

"Please!" Making a distasteful face, Ming dismissed that with a wave. "Sex with humans is so uncivil. No, there will be no raping, involuntary or otherwise. You are to be an employee of the kingdom while you document my life story. Guards; take Miss Purehart to the human resources department so she can be processed."

"And what if I refuse to work for you?" Resisting the robo-guards, she had fire in her eyes as she demanded an answer.

"As if that were ever a possibility." Shaking his head, Ming found her refusal humorous. "You are Miss Pollyanna Brianna Purehart, ace reporter for the Galactic Tribune. You do not have it within your capacity to refuse such a story as this."

Leaning down until he was almost face to face with the woman, he finished his thought.

"You, my lady, are a news-whore. According to my research, there is very little you wouldn't do for a headline like this. So I leave you to your empty display of resistance knowing full well that it is all merely an act."

There was something about the way he softened his words towards the end of his statement. It was not so much mocking as a frank assessment of her personality. And while she wanted desperately to deny the accusations, in truth he was absolutely right; *in no version of the multiverse would Polly Purehart ever let go of a front-page story like this.*

"If I work for you I will have no credibility in the media." She threw up the last roadblock she could think of.

"Oh, rest assured; the entire galaxy will know that you have been kidnapped by the time we reach DarSooth. Every inhabited system knows that you are now working under duress. Your credibility is fully intact. Though I doubt the same could be said for your virtue." Raising a single eyebrow, Ming looked into the distance. "Guards, take miss Purehart to employee orientation. Make sure that she sits in the front row. I wouldn't want her to miss any details of our benefits package."

Polly was just about to object one last time when the guards yanked her around towards Human Resources.

Standing over by the big windows of the great room, Ming and Lotus were eagerly discussing their plans of galactic domination. Motioning about with his hands as he spoke, the Emperor abruptly stopped and turned to face the cameraman.

"Well?" His voice went up an octave. "Why aren't you getting your employee credentials?"

Dave jumped slightly. Up until then he had been completely ignored by everyone.

"Me..?" He stammered, unsure if the previous offer had included him or just Polly.

"Young man, on this ship there are two kinds of people; those that work for me, and those that find themselves in a faulty airlock. Of which group would you prefer to be a member of?" As if explaining something to a child, Ming's voice took a falsetto tone as he patiently laid it out.

Imagining himself in an airlock as his eyes bugged out of their sockets, Dave knew which choice he would ultimately make. *But still, he had questions…*

"Do we get dental?" He asked sheepishly before an angry scowl from Ming sent him running for the door.

Wearing a skeptical look, Lotus looked after the young man.

"Are you sure he's Raven's *biological* child? Perhaps he was switched at the hospital…?" Looking back at his boss, the chief minion was having a hard time seeing the family resemblance. Raven had been an Amazonian goddess. *Dave was as far from godhood as you could get.*

Life as Minions

Polly was surprised at her new quarters. Being a network star she was used to elegant living, but this was some next level stuff. Her quarters included not only a magnificent suite, but an indoor pool, Zen garden, and a movie theater.

"This is all just for me?"

"Just you, no pets, no slaves, no undead sex orgies." Lotus responded with his nose in the air. "Your cameraman has his own apartment in steerage. The radiation down there is nothing that can't be treated with a little Ploraxine."

Standing a few feet away, Dave gulped at the thought of being irradiated while he slept. Turning around, Polly had a fiery look in her eyes.

"Absolutely not. You find him some radiation-free accommodations!" Hands on hips, she stood her ground.

"Fine...fine. We have a cell available..." He found himself cut off before he could tell them how nice their jail was. *Hardly any rats in the prison block...prisoners ate them all.*

"No! Find him an apartment that isn't a hazmat zone, or next door to the torture boxes." Her eyes sharpened as the journalist glared at the chief minion.

Shaking his head, Lotus was dismissive. "The torture boxes are clear over on the other side of the detention complex. Cell 2187 should be far enough away that he hardly smells the burning flesh."

"Do I need to talk to Ming?" Staring him down, she never flinched. While Lotus may have adorned himself with titles and jewelry, she knew that underneath it all he was just another sycophant loser. Nothing terrified him more than being tattled on to the boss.

"Oh, fine. I'll find him some standard quarters." He agreed. But behind his back he had his fingers crossed.

"HUMAN quarters." Polly specified by waving a finger. She had an idea the minion would try to pull something.

Giving a deep sigh, he agreed reluctantly. "Fine, human quarters that are not a cell or in a hazmat zone. How are you with radon gas?" Seeing their expressions, he waved off his own suggestion. "Never mind, I can house you in D-block. You'll get along famously there."

Alone in her new apartment, she was amazed that no expense had been spared. Clearly her abduction had not been a last-minute consideration. Ming had planned this for some time; that much was obvious by her suite. Even the closets and drawers were stocked with clothes in her exact size.

It amazed her; the places she could now get into with her employee credentials. Engineering, weapons, navigation…there seemed to be no limits. While the journalist found this tempting, she could not help but wonder why they would be allowed so much freedom.

"Sooo, what's on the schedule today?" Dave asked as he strolled up to the buxom journalist. Pausing to admire the way her clothes fit, he tried not to ogle. In the back of his mind he imagined her in one of the hero's outfits. *Oh, how great she would look in spandex!*

"War." Nodding, she looked up from the

tablet she had been reading.

"Naw, really. What're we doing today?" Laughing, the twenty-something cameraman assumed she had been joking.

"Really, really." She said as her lips formed a grimace. Holding up the tablet, she showed him the battle plans. "We are invading TorDal in an hour."

His face blanched as he saw that it was true. Stepping back a pace, he tried to minimize it all.

"Well…we'll be way back on the command ship, half a light-year from the shooting." Waving it off, he had just let a smile creep across his face when she tapped the screen again to reveal the details. Staring intently, the cameraman's eyes widened as Polly shattered his bubble.

"Yeah, no. We'll be in orbit during the battle." Sighing, she gave her assistant a frown. Really, she tended to look *through* Dave more than she looked AT him. It was something she frequently caught herself doing. She'd had many cameramen over the years. Male or female, they had all begun to blend in to one another. More than once she had called her assistants by the wrong name.

"We'll be…in low orbit?" Snatching the

tablet from her, Dave felt like he had been punched in the gut. "*Ooooh nooo*. This is not good, not good at all. We're providing direct fire support on the capital. We're gonna be right in the middle of the shit. Which way are the escape pods?"

"Forget it. They only work after they've been activated by the bridge. I checked already." Dismissing the idea with a shake of her head, she had no desire to waste time trying to reinvent the wheel.

Dave seemed crestfallen at this news. He spent a few seconds considering what lay ahead before he suddenly perked up.

"You checked the escape pods already?" He asked, seemingly out of the blue. "So if the pods had worked, you woulda left without me?"

"The network would provide me with a new cameraman." She replied, her face said she was serious. "How did you think you got this job? Saddle up; we have a story to cover."

Striding away towards the bridge, ace reporter Pollyanna Brianna Purehart fully intended to document the day. Behind her, Dave's mouth moved but no words came out. Struggling to come up with a way out of his fix, he could think of nothing viable.

"If I had a time machine, I'd go back in time and slap the living shit outta myself for taking this gig." His words spoke of his growing regret at accepting this assignment. The Chief Editor had convinced him it was a glamorous promotion, complete with a big red bow on top. Dave had been so distracted by the *shiny* that he had never even thought about why they would be offering him such a plum job.

Sagging, he picked up his camera equipment.

"Crewman number six; reporting for duty." He grumbled before following Polly into the Command Center.

As the deck shuddered beneath her feet, Polly gritted her perfect teeth while grasping the railing with one hand. Another plasma torpedo detonated short of the bridge, causing their whole world to shake violently. Despite the grave personal risk she faced, it was the dream of a third Emmy that kept her going. Feeling another blast-wave impact the ship, she was convinced that this would get her top honors this year.

But she'd had a hunch this time; an idea that could really put her reporting over the top. It had occurred to her that in the topsy-turvy chaos of a battle, there was one thing that she could count on to remain constant; *Ming's hubris*.

Really, it had seemed like an insane idea, asking Ming for an interview in the middle of a heated space battle. He was busy calling out orders, commanding the bridge minions, sending orders to the rest of the fleet…but nonetheless she had asked. Surprisingly, he raised an eyebrow and happily agreed. No doubt he thought it would frame him well to have the melee in the background.

"Why are you attacking the TorDal capital, unprovoked?" She thrust the microphone towards him. Really, with their technology there was no need for the unit in her hand. She simply preferred that method as a way to control the conversation.

"We are NOT attacking the scurrilous TorDal unprovoked. We are attacking them because they declared war against the empire this morning." Without even looking, he held out a hand to one side. A split second later Lotus had placed a tablet in his waiting grip. "Here is their formal declaration, filed legally through the Hague courts."

Polly was stunned for a moment as she looked over the document. His answer was unexpected. Mentally she shifted to a new angle of attack.

"But the TorDal had not yet attacked; you are drawing first blood here." She pointed out.

"But of course." He roared with a smile. "That is the nature of war. The TorDal were foolish to have declared without immediately attacking. Buffoons!"

Glancing back and forth between the document in her hand, and Ming, the reporter noticed a small detail.

"This time-stamp says that they declared war on you just five minutes before you dropped out of warp and began your assault?"

Shrugging, the man in the flowing red robes seemed indifferent. "I certainly was not going to wait around for them to attack first. When you declare war, you go to war, then and there! The TorDal seem to think that they could declare war, then have a nice cup of tea and contemplate things. No-no-no."

Shaking one of his bony fingers, he made it clear that the enemy had made the mistakes today. Standing there with flashes of cannon fire in the background made for an eerie image. It would have been perfect footage had it not been for the sound of Dave's sobbing in the background.

"Sire!" Tugging at his elbow, Lotus begged for his master's attention. "The TorDal have surrendered."

Ming was just about to launch into a lengthy detail of how he planned to crush his unworthy adversary when his chief minion interrupted him with the news of peace. Pausing as if he was taken aback, the dictator's eyebrows finally furrowed in anger.

"Well, did they declare a complete and unconditional surrender? Hmmm?" Raising his sharp eyebrows, Ming was not convinced.

"Uhhh," Lotus flipped through the documents. "Signed and notarized. Hey, they use Judy for a notary too."

Frowning as he made a fist, Ming had no interest in such petty details.

"Did they file the form two-dash-seventy-nine?" A murderous scowl had crossed his face as he demanded information from his chief minion.

"Uh…yes, sir, they did." Happily, Lotus

found the form properly completed.

"And did they digitally sign and stamp the nondisclosure form?" Waving a fist of death, Ming seethed as if he were seconds away from snapping.

"Uhhh, yes they did, filed and done in the Hague court." A bead of sweat ran down the minion's forehead.

It was as if someone had flipped a switch in Ming. Straightening up, he dropped the fist of death before giving a simple reply.

"Oh." His expression seemed a little glum. "War's over. Pack up the plasma cannons, box up the remaining missiles. Put the kill bots back in storage, and somebody call the clone factory and tell them they can cancel that big order. It looks like shore-leave in Boca this weekend, eh boys?"

There was a cheer around the bridge crew as they thought of how much fun it would be to invade a beachside community.

"That's it?" Polly seemed surprised, especially when Ming turned around with a beer in his hand.

"Yeah. War's over. They filed the right papers."

"I thought you were the man who only followed his own brand of law?" Raising an eyebrow, she was sure she had him cornered this time.

"This **is** my law. I enacted it in in…thirty two? I always felt you should be able to turn off a war just as fast as you started it." Nodding at his own logic, Ming took a swig from the bottle in his hand. Turning to cheer his bridge crew, there was loud applause from the minions there.

"This is Pollyanna Purehart reporting from the bridge of the *Mors Machina*. You saw it here first; on Channel 9 news at nine."

D-block

As much as Dave hated going back to his quarters in D-block, he had to get some sleep. It had been a long day of murder and destruction and he just needed to drink some scotch and pass out for 8 to 10 hours.

But that was the rub; his roommate was not interested in sleeping. In fact, none of the soldiers billeted in D-block wanted to sleep tonight. After all, they had just defeated the TorDal, and currently sped towards the Bali star system for some R&R. Nope, tonight was party-night in D-block!

Tall, brown, and lumpy, the battle

minions were one of the ugliest creatures the cameraman had ever seen. The first time he saw one of Ming's galactic marines out of their battle armor, he thought they looked like a walking pile of malignant tumors. They were simply hideous.

And then there was the smell...

It was commonly believed that Ming had manufactured the marines in a lab. But in truth, the soldiers were from the BelRuet system. The Morganeese were a unisex, heavy-world species, adapted to life in very thin atmospheres. Really they were the perfect soldiers, and their entire culture reflected it. They were a warrior race, and working for Ming had always been a natural fit; they enjoyed killing, and Ming had lots of people that needed to be killed. *It had been symbiosis from the start.*

"Boss man pay real good, y'know." Bottie said as he downed another gallon of kerosene. Pausing, the marine thumped his chest until he burped a red fireball of gas.

"Holy shit!" Dave cringed in the corner as his hair was singed by the belch.

"Oooh, sorry puny *hey-u-man.*" Laughing, the corporal sitting on the other side of Dave gave him a shove that sent his head into one of Bottie's brick-like shoulders.

"Hmmmppph." Sitting in the corner, another marine showed his disapproval by shaking his tumors. "If we ever invade Earth, we will need to be careful or we will break all of the humans."

The marines hooted in unison before banging their heads together as they chanted their unit ditty.

"Mo ha mak-mar. Make the cut, spill their gut, mo ha mak-mar!" Cheering as they finished, the one nearest the door took a moment to turn up the stereo even louder. Between the shouting and the shriek of the music, it was impossible to hear.

"Careful for the *hey-u-man*!" Bottie slapped one of the marines who was crowding Dave too much. "Boss man want this one good and alive."

"So he can eat him?" The Corporal imagined the human on a platter with some potatoes, and maybe some Fava beans.

"Nooo, de boss do not eat him." Bottie laughed openly at the junior noncom.

"I would eat him." Shrugging, Corporal Aileeek failed to see the logic of **not** eating the human.

"Could we not talk about eating me for one night, please?" Dave was at his wits end. After a week in D-block, he had begun to reconsider that room down in steerage. *Lotus did say the radiation was treatable…*

Bigger than the rest by a third, Bottie's laugh easily droned out the other marines. Clapping a heavy hand on Dave's back practically knocked the fillings out of his teeth.

"We not eat you, Daaaave of channel nine. Yoo have nothing worry 'bout." His thunderous laugh echoed around the small room.

"But you have eaten humans before, haven't you?" Giving his roomie a sharp look, he asked something that had been bothering him since he arrived.

"Eat *hey-u-man*? Only in restaurant." Bottie waved a hand as if that made it okay.

"I eat a *hey-u-man* once on Thaxor." The private in the doorway admitted. "It was tasty, but I did not care for the fibrous coverings."

The others looked back and forth between the private and Dave before they understood what he meant.

"Those just clothes!" Bottie broke out

laughing.

"You 'spose take clothes off before eat them. Like banana, peel and eat." Also laughing, the Corporal lambasted his newest recruit.

"Yeahhhh, we're still talking about eating Dave…" The cameraman pointed out weakly as the soldiers began discussing favorite recipes. While they were primarily known for their warrior skills, the Morganeese were also renowned for their cuisine. After all, they were a species that ate practically everything they encountered, so it only followed that they would know a lot of ways to cook a thing. *A fact that did not make Dave feel any safer.*

"So…" Changing the subject, Dave took the conversation in another direction. "How do you guys like working for Ming?"

"Good medical and dental." Bottie opened his maw to reveal row after row of sharp daggers that were his teeth. "I could bite through a BelNor in a single bite!"

Snapping his jaw shut, the big guy demonstrated. For his part, Dave was trying to find a way to shrink even further into the corner, and away from that giant maw of teeth.

"We get to kill lots. I like that. Every week, someone new to slay." Nodding, the Corporal showed contentment.

"Yah, but we stop short today, like cowardly little Vootogs!" The private showed disdain.

"What you say?" Perking up, the noncom gave his subordinate a wary look.

"That was *shite*, we stopping the attack jus' because dey file some papers. We Morganeese, we should crush anyone who dare declare war. Teach dem, make example of dem. Wipe dem out." Grinding a fist in his open palm, the private envisioned how the TorDal home world would have looked after they irradiated it with fission weapons.

"Dat not smart way to fight." Dismissing it, the Corporal set about to explain it to the *noob*. "Yoo see, you kill entire planet den we not make any money off dat planet. War cost much money. No money, no more war. Dem papers say day give us all they money so we can afford to go fight more peoples."

"Kill all enemy and no one left to fight." Bottie nodded as he explained the point.

"Oooooh." The rookie seemed to be experiencing an epiphany. "That good idea."

"Heh," The Corporal gave a guffaw. "I

like shoot TorDal in butt with disruptor so I can watch face as they disintegrate. Very funny dat!"

Horrified, Dave watched as they each compared combat footage they had recorded that morning. Rendered in vivid 3D, the footage captured every grotesque detail as they beat, burned, and bludgeoned the local populous of the capital city. As bad as the footage was, the worst part of it all was the way the marines laughed when they watched the video. The mayhem seemed to truly fascinate them. It reminded him of human men watching football.

"That's a kill!" Standing upright, the Corporal enthusiastically cheered for the scene of Bottie crushing an entire family under his mighty boot. "Oh, lookie, you got some Tor on you boot. I hope you clean dem off before you came in da house."

There was a laugh all around from the soldiers as they downed their drinks. Wedged in the corner between Bottie and the Corporal, Dave could think of no way to extricate himself. It was clear that there was no sleep to be had here. He intended to beg Polly to let him sleep on her couch…if only he could get out of that room.

"The *hey-u-man* does not understand our joy for the fight." Bottie explained to his cohorts.

"ShrekNar." The Corporal said the single word. Immediately there was recognition around the room.

"ShrekNar." Bottie agreed with a broad smile.

I don't suppose ShrekNar is Morganeese for sleep, is it?" Feeling a sinking sensation in his stomach, he did not like the way they were acting.

"Look, we can just order pizza. I'll pay." Worried that he was about to become dinner, Dave offered the logical deal.

"ShrekNar." The Corporal said with a nod before grabbing Dave. Being held aloft by an iron grip, the cameraman could only see glimpses of the world as he was carried out of the room and down three levels. Once there, he felt someone force a helmet onto his head and an energy-sword into his hand. After that he was unceremoniously dropped into an open enclosure.

"Oh no." His words were nearly inaudible as he realized he was standing in some kind of gladiator ring. His mind was just wondering what beast he was to face when the door behind him opened.

What stepped out was a cross between a wolf and a nightmare. Jet black, with eyes that glowed from deep sockets, the creature's frame spoke of fantastic speed and power. Clearly, this was a killing machine.

The sound of soldiers cheering was deafening as the creature approached without hesitation. Extending its toothed snout, the beast was within just a few inches when the cameraman gave a shriek. Like a flash, he swung the sword in a flaming arc, right through the beast. With barely a yip, the nightmarish creature fell to the ground in two quivering pieces.

The cheering immediately turned to a stunned rebuke. Many were silent, but most took a few seconds to utter a curse.

"He killed da dog?" The Corporal was aghast.

"What kind of..." another soldier showed open disdain.

A hail of red solo cups and chicken bones rained down on him as the crowd expressed its displeasure.

"What the shite?" Dave could not understand their revulsion. "You put me here in a ring, with a sword in my hand, against the most vile beast imaginable…and you're pissed because I won?" Sword in hand, the photographer was feeling cocky after slaying the beast.

"No, no." Bottie gave a grimace as he tried to explain. "Dog to help human defeat Nar. You jus' kill puppy!"

Looking down, he had just started to feel the pain of having murdered an innocent dog when something occurred to him.

"But…if that wasn't the beast I was supposed to fight…" Gesturing with his sword, he heard the big doors behind him begin to creak open. Petrified, his feet seemed welded in place. His legs refused to run, even as he could hear the massive creature dragging itself closer and closer behind him.

Finally he could bear it no more. Turning, he found himself facing a beast so large that he stood in its shade. With giant buggy eyes and a round proboscis where its mouth should have been, it looked as if it could easily suck his blood like a milkshake. Past that there were the massive wings that spread out behind it like a fighter jet. Standing on thick, hairy legs, the creature stood almost directly over him.

"Ooooooohhhh." Was all he could say. He had been expecting something bigger than the puppy, but this was a whole other level of big. Roughly the size of an executive jet, he doubted he would be much more than a snack to this hideous freak of nature.

Pausing, the thing began tilting its head down to examine the cameraman. Slowly unrolling the proboscis, it seemed to be preparing to attack.

"Yaaaaahhh!" With a guttural shriek, Dave thrust the sword forward, driving it into the space between those big, bulging eyes. Still shrieking his death cry, the cameraman felt like he was on autopilot the way his hands automatically carried out the act. In his own mind he had already shut down, so it surprised him to see the beast giving its last mortal scream before crashing to the ground with a dusty thud.

Just like before when he had killed the puppy, there was a long silence. But this time when they finally began shouting, the voices were cheering FOR the cameraman. Steadily there were more and more calls for *Camam Dave* as they applauded him in drunken revelry. He had tried to correct that last part, but to no avail. *Cameraman* was only his profession, not his name, and they continually mispronounced that.

"ShekNar!" Holding up a mighty fist, Bottie called out the single word.

"ShekNar!" The rest of the marines echoed his sentiment.

"Yeah, ShekNar all around." Dave's sarcasm was evident, right up until he passed out. Crumpling to the ground in a heap, his sword went clattering across the deck.

"Oh shit, mon." The Corporal declared as he looked over the prone cameraman. "I tink we broke the *hey-u-man*. De boss man is gonna be mad as hell."

"C'mon, wake the hell up." Polly snapped her fingers in front of his face. "Don't give me any excuses about not sleeping."

"They made me slay a beast." He spoke as if in a dream-state. "It was…"

"It was a giant moth. I saw it." She frowned. "I don't think it even has any offensive capabilities."

"It was a beast…so big…" Still staring into the distance, Dave's hands clumsily handled the camera.

"You killed a bug. Get over it." Hands on

hips, the curvy journalist evaluated her cameraman. "Today we're interviewing refugees from the Calit system."

"Calit…?" He repeated the word as if it was meaningless.

"Calit, the star system Ming paved over to build his intragalactic freeway, millions of souls lost when he turned their star into a black hole. You remember that place?" She derided him before striding towards the waiting shuttle.

"Can I sleep on the way down?" He whined before following. As tired as he was, he could not resist the opportunity to ogle Polly from behind. Truly, her curvy shape was pure art. With his eyes fixed on her butt, he plodded along in a stupor as they boarded the ship. Once buckled into his seat, he was out like a light.

"So your family lived on Drechau for how many generations?" Polly's perfect blue eyes were sympathetic as she leaned in with the microphone. Her golden locks of hair flowed down her shoulders like a waterfall.

"Forty-seven." The Calit woman supplied that information readily.

"And you were just forced off your land, told to get out or die?" Centering the microphone between the husband and wife, she opened up the question to both.

"Told us to get out, and that anyone still there would be killed when the sun was snuffed out. Such a tragedy." Misses Milner shook her head as her mouth curved down into a frown.

"But the compensation package was not bad." The husband spoke up for the first time. "It was enough that we could afford to retire and travel the galaxy in a recreational vehicle."

"It's a sixty-footer." The wife leaned forward as if revealing a secret. "We're waiting for it to be delivered here now."

Polly seemed surprised at this. "You're not refugees…like the others?"

Gesturing to the other people who seemed to be camped out around the area, she had assumed that the couple was in the same dire straits.

"Refugees?" The couple gave that a shared chuckle.

"But you're…?" She was unsure of the politically correct way to phrase it. "You're all stranded here in this refugee camp?"

The Milners found this wildly amusing. Again sharing a laugh they pointed at Polly's expression. Frustrated, she was about to turn away when the husband finally explained.

"They are not refugees. Those are the Sholveks; their ship is in the shop. The mechanic has a part on order. The next three families are all waiting for the luxury cruise liner Eldorfa. Next to them are the Cardona clan; they just could not get reservations at a local motel. There are more of us than rooms in this town, so we wait in this friendly zone. They have coffee and donuts here." Shrugging, he laid it all out for her.

"The compensation package was quite generous, what with the exchange rate and all." Missus Milner testified with a smile. "You should see the kitchen in my new home."

"But what about all of the people who were killed when the star was destroyed?" Polly knew that was sure to be a flash point.

"Oh, that is indeed a tragedy." Mister Milner said as his wife nodded in agreement. "Very bad news."

"Did you know many people who were killed when it happened?" Digging deeper, Polly could smell the blood in this story.

"Oooh, well…" The man stood stiffly as he gave that a thought. Exchanging a series of looks with his wife, Mister Milner suggested someone. "Well, there was Glowena and Connor?"

"Nope, jiggled me the other day. They're part owners of a resort in Praxis." Missus Milner waved aside that suggestion.

"But then there was Bilby?" He put forth the suggestion.

"Belen. Lives in a custom-made tree house now."

"Oh. Well what about Thad and Claxia?" He was sure he had her this time.

"Earth. They got a job probing humans. Good benefits." She nodded.

"I always said she had the fingers to be a prober." Mister Milner nodded his head enthusiastically. "Didn't I tell her that?"

Polly's soft expression had turned to frustration. "So did you two actually know anyone at all that was killed when the star was collapsed?"

There was a long pause as the spouses exchanged silent looks. Finally Mister Milner shrugged casually. "No, I guess not."

"You have to understand, it was a good deal." The wife insisted. "I have a marble bathtub. The spigots are all gold plated. Can you believe that?"

"But your planet?" Polly persisted.

"Meh." The husband waved a hand. "The star was becoming unstable anyhow. Three times last year we had solar flares take out the entire grid. The fission rate was increasing and the thing was going to start expanding any year now. Lots of folks were already moving out before Ming told us to get out. The storms were terrible."

"The carpet is three inches deep…" Again Missus Milner pretended to whisper.

Turning to the camera, Polly finally broke character.

"Okay, let's wrap it up for now." Using a hand, she gave the cut sign.

Days later…

Looking distraught, Polly stormed out of her apartment and nearly ran headlong into Dave. Backing up in a huff, she straightened her clothes. Giving her cameraman a scowl, she was in no mood to socialize.

"The interview today is cancelled, I have to go somewhere." She started to move past him.

"That's what I was coming to tell you. Ming cancelled the interview…" Dave was cut off.

"And I have to get to Plaxair." She added. "By ten AM local."

"Odd…we're in orbit over Plaxair now." There was a curious tone to Dave's voice as he said it. "What exactly is it you need to do down there?"

Polly seemed to find the coincidence odd as well. "Why are we here?"

"Dunno." Dave simply shrugged. "Ming does what Ming does. That's part of being the evil galactic dictator; you can do pretty much whatever you want. So again, what do YOU have to do down on Plaxair?"

She regarded him for a moment before finally speaking. "Today is Captain Chaos' funeral. I just found out from Legend."

"The Cap died?" Dave's eyes sank as he sagged to the nearest wall. "He was my favorite when I was growing up. He was sooo cool, you never knew what kind of crap he was gonna pull. Oh *maaaan*, I can't believe he's really gone!"

"Wonderful, I'm sorry for your loss. I have to go." Stepping around him, she started to move on before he grabbed her arm.

"Wait a minute there. You gotta take me as your plus-one." He insisted with a nod.

"No I don't." Breaking away, she headed down the hallway.

"No, seriously; you have gotta take me. When I was a kid, Captain Chaos was my hero. I even had a Captain Chaos lunchbox for three years." Jumping in front of her, the photojournalist begged her to reconsider.

"Lots of kids had Captain Chaos lunchboxes." Dismissing his claims, she never even slowed down.

"I was in college." He made a funny face as he admitted that fact.

"It's a private affair." She countered without breaking pace. Ahead of her Dave continued to hop along backwards while he tried to implore her to change her mind.

"Pweeeeze Jessica!"

"NO!" Her shout echoed down the immaculate hallway.

"You're gonna change your m-iii-nd." He said in a sing-songy fashion. Finally stopping to let her pass, he watched her slam open the doors to the hanger bay as she entered.

"I said no, and if you ask again, you're fired." Seething, she glanced back at him with eyes that could sever an artery.

Stopping short, his smile never faded. Dave simply slowed to a saunter and enjoyed the view from behind. Grinning, he watched as Polly strode up to the nearest guard.

"I need a ship." She said in a firm voice.

"Tain't no-oone." Shrugging, the guard seemed indifferent. Looking over he spotted the cameraman and perked up. "Dave, what up *hay-u-man*."

"Dax, dood! I thought you had the day off with the rest of Delta." Exchanging a fist-bump, Dave greeted the soldier he knew from the housing block.

"I did, but some ass-hole get drunk, shoot up the showers, cause lot damage. And **me** get blame for it." Nodding, he did not seem terribly angry about it.

"But Dax, **you were** the one who got drunk and shot up the washroom, and shot off Bottie's little toe, and set fire to the cleaning closet…" Trying to be delicate as he said it, Dave did not want to anger the lumbering soldier. Even their love-taps were akin to being punched by Mike Tyson.

"Yeah, I thought da charges sounded a little familiar." He agreed solemnly.

"Hello!" Snapping her fingers in front of his face, Polly showed obvious irritation. "I need a ship."

"There no ship, 'cept mebbe dat one." He shook his tumors in the direction of a small craft that sat dripping fluid onto the deck.

"Fine." Exasperated, the reporter waved it off. Surely it had to be safe, despite appearances, or they would never have offered it to her. *At least that was her assumption based on her own bloated self-value.*

"But no pilot to fly itt." Dax dismissed her request before turning back to Dave. "Ja hear 'bout Marley and Crispey dancing the nasty-dance in the laundry room last night? Ehhh?"

"And I bet ya six clavu that it was Crispey doing the bending." Dave's tone was derisive as they gossiped.

"I always say Crispey is a bender. I tell him, yoo Crispey, you is a bender. But he always say he is a straightee, but now we see; he is a bendy." Oblivious of Polly's angry eyes boring through him, Dax had slumped up against a bulkhead as he exchanged gossip with the cameraman.

"We'll see which one files for maternity leave, that'll tell us who's the bendy. Right?" Laughing, Dave seemed genuinely amused by the happenings of Dogpatch. While it had been rough at first, he had gotten used to bunking with the soldiers…*mostly*.

"Excuuuuuse me!" Polly muscled her tiny frame in between Dave and Dax. Standing with her hands on buxom hips, she looked up into the guard's eyes. "You need to find me a pilot, and you need to do it now. I am a personal guest of Ming, and I am to be afforded whatever resources I need. It's written in my contract."

She had lied about the contract, but the rest was true. Ming had made an announcement that she was to be treated like a royal guest. (*For Dave, he had simply asked that no one kill or maim the cameraman during his stay.*)

"T'aint none. All da pilots all left with the shuttles. Everyone gone on shore leave, 'cept assholes what shoot up da washroom." Seemingly indifferent, Dax could see no reason for concern. Unless there was some killing to be done, he didn't see the point of most things that happened on this ship. Some may have called him simplistic, but Dax preferred to think of himself as having a singular focus; fighting, drinking, fucking. Aside from that, it was all felgerkarb to the hulking guard.

"Then you need to call Ming himself and get me a pilot!" Poking him in one of his tumors, she did not even flinch at touching the bulbous flesh.

"Can't." Again with the shrug, Dax was about to turn away when she poked him again.

"Why not?"

"Ummm," He seemed to process it in his head before completing the thought. "Ming gone, him left this morning early. Said he had a date."

"Ooooh, I bet he's meeting Wanda Wicked!" Nodding his approval, Dave knuckle-bumped Dax again as they shared a chuckle. "And we know who'll be doing all the bending on *that* date, eh?"

"Yeah mon." Chuckling, the henchman was well familiar with the woman who was known to literally swing into their lives aboard the *Mors Machina*. It was not unheard of for the villainess to blow the front doors off the hinges just to make an entrance.

"Someone must be running the ship. Call your chain of command and get me a pilot!" Fuming, it felt like a personal insult to her to be left stranded like this.

"S'okay." Dax touched the side of his head and began talking to his next in command. Babbling back and forth in their native tongue, their dialog was incomprehensible to the humans who watched. After a few minutes of heated exchange, a second screen opened up to reveal another of the security force. This one sported three white hash-marks, as opposed to the first supervisor's two hash-marks.

Again the debate went back and forth as one explained to another, nearly verbatim to the first time. Even the arguing and yelling sounded nearly identical. Then finally a third screen opened up. This security officer had 4 hash-marks on his uniform.

"OMG…how much longer can this go on…?" Polly groaned.

"Well, see that guy who just popped up?" Dave asked in a low voice. "He's a corporal. Now you have five grades of NCO, followed by six more grades of officer before you get to the Captain of the ship…" He did a poor job of hiding his glee at her discomfort.

"Crap noodles!" She shouted as she turned away. Grumbling angrily, she sounded like a Dodge with a timing issue. Standing with her back to them, she chose to wait it out in solitude. In no mood for small talk, it was simply easier for her to be rude and turn her back on Dave then engage with him. Besides, he was just her lowly cameraman. *They were all little people, nothing worthy of influencing her chi*

It took a half hour before they finally got past the captain, who seemed downright fearful of the idea of this getting back to Ming. Instead he patched them through to one final source.

"Hello?" Clearly irritated, Lotus sat staring into the screen. Gone was his long, greasy hair. In its place was a perfectly shaved head. On the side was the unmistakable sign of toilet paper sticking to a shave-cut.

"I need a pilot, IMMEDIATELY!" Finally rejoining the conversation, Polly was adamant. Looking down at her watch, she was getting angrier by the minute.

"We don't have any." He shrugged before repeating the very same information they had heard from the previous 16 contestants. "They all left with the transports for shore leave."

"Then recall one, train one, pull a minion out of the freezer…I don't care! I just need a pilot to fly me, in **that** pathetic little ship, down to the surface of the planet. Is that asking too much from the mighty Ming Dynasty?"

Keeping a poker face, Lotus tolerated her. Although he found her visually stunning, he had never really cared for the woman personally. It was for this reason that the Polly Purehart sex-bot he kept in the closet was set for mute. He liked to look at her, but her voice grated on his nerves. By his reckoning she was simply another outsider, sympathetic to the goals of their enemies.

"Contrary to popular belief, we do not manufacture or clone our pilots, they come from one-hundred percent USDA approved academies. And we currently have none until noon." He pretended to be polite, though he was mostly trying to look at her boobs.

Lotus was about to switch off and go visit the sex-bot in the closet when he noticed something on his screen.

"Isn't that your cameraman Donald?" He asked, jabbing a crooked finger at the image.

"Dave." The photojournalist corrected him.

"Have him fly you, he's academy trained. Why in the Zorbal are you bothering me?"

Showing disgust on his face, Lotus switched off the screen.

Polly was taken aback as she tried to process that. Turning slowly, she faced her subordinate with a scowl.

"What exactly did he mean by academy trained?"

"Well, it means that I completed LARS level six flight certification, and hold a current ATP license, with heavy-world endorsements." He was just about to list some of his other qualifications when she cut him off.

"This whole time we wasted talking to one minion after another...and you were a pilot all along? Why didn't you say anything?" Her eyes narrowed to slits, there was not an ounce of sugar or spice in her veins at that moment.

"Well, I was gonna, but my boss said she'd fire me if I asked again, so technically I was prohibited from telling you." Smug in his delivery, Dave shared a laugh with Dax.

"Don't get funny with me, Mister!" She jabbed a finger in his face. "You are going to fly me down to the surface, right now."

"Can't." Acting innocent, he gave a dramatic pause before answering. "I'm off today. My boss ordered me to take a vacation day. I have proof:" He waved a hand to display the footage from earlier.

"Take the day off, that's an order!" She could be seen yelling over her shoulder just before the camera panned down for a close-up of her bottom.

"Actually…" He started out gleefully. "I was thinking of doing some shopping. Say, Dax, since I'm a certified pilot, there wouldn't be any problem with me signing out that shuttle over there for a trip down to the surface for the afternoon?"

"Nope, not as long as ya' brings back some beer." Grinning, the big soldier could think of a lot of places he would rather be than on guard duty.

"Yeahhhh, no. You're on restriction and Bottie would beat us both silly if I brought you any beer. But I'm still gonna take the shuttle." Giving a wink, Dave turned to head towards the shuttle.

It was what happened next that was a complete surprise. Dave was just starting towards the shuttle when Polly moved around in front of him and delivered a stunning right-cross that sent him spinning onto the ground.

Looking up from the ground, Dave was more stunned than injured. Although she had knocked him down, it had really just been the surprise of it all. That's not to say that she didn't know how to deliver a punch; her fist had turned him into a bobblehead for a few seconds there.

"You punched me?" He muttered a curse under his breath. "You can't do that to employees!"

"*Au contraire*!" She waved a manicured finger. "Thanks to Ming's deregulation, I can do anything I want, up to and including selling your kidneys."

Advancing on the man, she pantomimed the act of ripping out his organs, one at a time.

"Oooh!" Dave realized she was right. The company handbook stipulated only that they could not *intentionally* kill employees. Accidental death and dismemberment were merely frowned upon.

"Now get off your ass and fly me down to that planet before you wake up in a bathtub full of ice." Her voice had turned to a hiss as she used a sharp fingernail to lift his chin until they were eye to eye.

Although he was genuinely fearful of

what she might do, there was also something so familiar about her manner. It was such a stark departure from her normal wholesome persona that people saw on TV. Yet, there was something about it he just couldn't put his finger on. Scuttling to his feet, he finally winked at her.

"Toldja you'd wanna take me with you." He kidded her before boarding the shuttle.

Taking one last look at the greasy exterior of the craft, Polly was having reservations about the trip. *Was it normal for stuff to leak out of the manifolds that way?* Shaking her head, she boarded, slamming the hatch behind her just so the world would know she was still mad about being late.

Although they arrived together, with Dave officially as her plus-one, they were soon separated as Polly was ushered to prime seating just behind the family. Dave quickly found himself standing way in the back with the schmucks.

Originally it had been an ordinary funeral, just a family mourning its loss. But once word of the deceased's secret identity became public, the affair blew-up into a full-fledged event. Not only were there thousands of fans, reporters, and assorted lookie-loos, but also a few hundred police officers providing crowd control and traffic support. Some were there in official capacity, others simply came to honor the fallen hero who had helped them battle crime in these very streets. Although it had been a few years, the city still had fond memories of Captain Chaos defeating MegaLord in hand to hand combat, right there in the city plaza. That had been a glorious day indeed, and every frame captured on film for posterity.

There was the usual speechmaking by various celebrities. Captain Petrol gave a eulogy that strayed into references to his corporate sponsors. After that the Mayor babbled on in *politesse* for half an hour…

Although most people were growing bored with the lengthy service, Dave was as happy as a child on Christmas morn. From his vantage at the back of the chapel he could pick out no fewer than twelve active supers, and another ten retired. It was the single biggest collection of super heroes he had ever seen in his life. *Why, if Ming knew about this event, all he would have to do is nuke the site, and all of his problems would be gone in a single flash of light,* he thought to himself.

Craning his head around, the cameraman was surprised to see a familiar face standing in the cheap seats behind him. Feeling a sense of giddiness, there was no way he couldn't recognize Max Impact. Even without the costume, and about 40 years older, Dave was 200% sure it was him. His face had been on every box of Wheaties for a year straight after the battle of planet Costco. Although Ming had defeated him in the end, the battle had been epic, and destroyed much of the Reichmann center. Granted, the old building was just days away from a scheduled demolition. But still, it was the event that had once inspired the photojournalist to want to be a hero too. Dave could not count how many times his cape had gotten tangled in the bicycle chain before he gave up the dream. His mother had been right; he was just not cut out for the hero business.

Giving a little salute, Dave tried to let the incognito hero know that his secret was safe with him. For his own part Max was simply wondering who the rubbernecking kid was.

Dave tried to resist the urge to keep

looking back, but he had to. It was Max Impact; the guy who had invented the Super-Mega-Power-Punch. *OMG, he was like three feet away!* He just had to look again.

But rather than be totally obvious, Dave decided to turn and look from the other direction this time. Bending around, Dave glanced over the faces that listened to the eulogy. Fat woman, skinny guy, hairy guy, strange looking bald guy, and Max Impact. Sighing, he finally began to turn away when his eyes stalled on the bald guy standing next to Max. There was something familiar about his eyes.

Slightly shorter than Dave, the bald man looked like a fifty-something insurance adjustor or some other denizen of the suburbs. His clothes spoke of a working stiff, and his pasty complexion said he rarely saw sun. Really he was about the most nondescript person in the room...so why did he stand out so much? *It was the eyes, something about the eyes.* Oddly, the bald guy reminded him of Ming, but without the elaborate beard and crimson robes.

Turned back around front again, Dave pondered the question until he spotted Omega Girl in the front row with the widow.

After that he completely forgot about the old guy.

Mmmmm, Omega Girl…

Most of the trip back to the *Mors Machina* passed without a word. Polly's anger from that morning had subsided during the service and left her in a reflective mood.

"I thought you went to college? You never mentioned the academy." Speaking for the first time in hours, she looked her cameraman over with a skeptical eye.

"Technically, the academy IS college." Sidestepping the real question, he was intentionally evasive. Besides, he was feeling dejected after striking out with Omega Girl.

"But if you went to the academy, then why aren't you an officer right now, serving in the forces somewhere in the galaxy?" Sitting up a little, the reporter activated the in-dash coffee dispenser. *Really it was just a Keureg.*

"I went to flight school to be a pilot, but you have to be a natural born killer to do that job, so apparently that lets me out." He scowled at the end as if it were his fault.

"I thought you just had to be able to fly?" The reporter was unsure if he was being literal or figurative.

"Nah, they have this test called the *Nati Interfectorem* that can determine if you have the will to kill or not. See, the fleet doesn't wanna spend all that money on a shiny little Tar32 deep-space fighter if you're not going to use it to kill everything you come across. So I failed the *Nati* trials and got booted out."

Raising a blonde eyebrow, Polly's interest had been piqued. This was the first she had ever heard of the *Nati Interfectorem* test. The concept interested her.

"How exactly does this test work?"

"Oh," He laughed nervously. "They hook up a buncha leads to you, including a couple on your junk. Then you fly through this shoot/don't-shoot scenario. I naturally assumed that you were supposed to shoot the bad guys, but not things like school buses and hospitals. But apparently I was wrong. The guys who shot everything that moved got promoted up to weapons school. One guy even shot up his own simulated base. That guy is a squadron leader now." Making a funny face, Dave was able to elicit a tiny giggle from his boss.

"But you killed the Nar beast, or whatever it was? Doesn't that mean you have the killer instinct?"

This time it was Dave who gave a laugh. "But that was just a giant moth, wasn't it?"

Turning away, Polly felt a little embarrassed. "The pictures made it look smaller than it really was."

Dave cackled openly before explaining. "Nah. Turns out it really was just a big space-moth that Bottie found in a storage locker. Me killing it was standard self defense; not the same thing as the *Nati Interfectorem*. Bottom line; I'm just not cut out to be a mad-dawg killer."

"Hmmph. In the moth world you're right up there with the bug zapper on their scale of evil." She pointed out.

"Oh yes, I'm a regular Dave the Merciless of Insectopia." Screwing his face up into an evil grin, he did his best impression of the dictator. "I shall squash you, and crush you, and exfoliate you, and disassemble you down to your very atoms until nothing remains of you but a greasy spot!"

Finishing his skit by holding up the double *fists of death* truly captured the essence of their ruler. It was as if everything he did absolutely required overacting. The laughs finally tapered off as something occurred to Dave.

"Y'know, I coulda swore I saw a guy who could be Ming's body double at the funeral. A little shorter than the real guy, but same eyes, same bald chrome-dome. Even had that mole over the left eye." Something stopped him in his thinking as he looked Polly in the eyes. "You don't think it coulda been…?"

"Ming?" Her expression said she thought he was being an idiot. Actually, that was her default expression whenever she was dealing with the cameraman. "That's crazy. We're lucky he didn't air-bomb the site when word of the gathering leaked. I'm convinced the only reason he didn't is because I was there. If I'd skipped the ceremony, he may have wiped out everyone there."

For his part, Dave resisted the urge to point out her narcissism in that statement. But really, it was in line with everything he had seen since he started working for the woman. There seemed to be considerable daylight between her public image and reality. Turning away, he was starting to think she was nothing more than a pretty shell.

Fidgeting with their course, he had just made a minor navigational correction when the entire system went black. Around them all of the lights blinked out, leaving them in inky blackness until the emergency lights finally enabled. Feeling anxious, Dave knew something catastrophic must have happened for all systems to wink out like that.

"What did you do?" Irritated, Polly was sure it was something her pilot had done.

"Not me." Dave held his hands above the panel. He was just about to further defend his piloting skills when they heard it.

At first it was just the sound of something impacting the outside of the ship. Not a collision, but like something heavy had just attached itself to the hull. There was a brief moment of silence, then they felt the first footstep, then the second step, as it dragged itself across the metal skin of the ship.

Polly gave a little shriek as her hand reflexively covered her mouth. Cringing in her seat, she sat wide-eyed and staring at a moving spot on the ceiling.

Beside her Dave was scrambling to make sense of what was happening. His best guess was either Bortas or pirates. But Bortas would already be eating the metal hull and multiplying by the thousands, so that meant it was pirates. Unfortunately, the anti-pirate defensive system was powered by the main bus, which was down. So regardless of what was out there, he was absolutely powerless to stop it.

Step by step, they could hear the creature dragging its swarthy mass across the metal plating above their heads. It sounded hideous and vile as it seemed to take its time edging closer and closer to the main window. In their seats, Dave and Polly both pushed themselves back into their seats just to put some distance between themselves and the main window. From the sound of its steps, it would be visible through the glass any second now…

"BAAAAHHHHH" It appeared in a blur, a round orb attached to a body. In a flash it smacked into the windshield and stayed there. With its head pinned against the glass, they could actually hear the loud bellowing sound it emitted. "WAHAHAHAHAHAH!"

This time it was Dave who screamed the loudest. With a shriek that only space dogs could have heard, he drew a strange look from Polly. But more importantly, they had both begun to notice something about the creature.

"Oh." Polly gave a smile of relief. "It's Mister Marvelous."

It took a split second for Dave to realize it was true, but once he did his heart beat even faster. There he could see for himself, the big, purple **M** on the side of his helmet. It was a logo the cameraman knew well, having once worn it for six consecutive Halloweens. He would have gone another year as the superhero but his mother finally threw away the smelly old costume.

Still laughing inside of his helmet, Mister Marvelous gave a wink at the pair before disappearing out of sight. A few seconds later and power was restored to the main bus. Blinking in the bright light, they were unsure what he was up to until they heard the airlock cycling.

"He's coming aboard??" Dave's eyes opened so wide they nearly fell out of his head. Breathless, he felt as if he had waited his entire life for this moment. He had met the man three other times, but those were just fan events or book signings. This would be totally different; he could feel it.

Beside him, Polly regarded her subordinate with a hint of disdain. It seemed odd to her to see a grown man gushing so much over another man. Really she thought it a little creepy. Honestly, she could have better understood it if it had been a gay-crush. But she knew full well that the cameraman was just an ordinary, garden variety, fan-boy.

A split second before the hatch opened, Polly straightened her shirt and switched to smile-mode. She was so pretty when she gave that delicate smile, like a dainty little southern belle. While there were feminists who would have decried how she used her sexuality to manipulate, Polly considered it her Midas-touch; *everything she touched with that smile turned to gold.*

"Polly, my girl!" All smiles, Mister Marvelous had his helmet folded back as he exchanged hugs with the woman.

"Marv!" She called him by her own personal pet name. Giving him a good squeeze, she made it seem like they were old friends.

"Hey little girly-girl, what're you doing clear out here?" Stepping back, Mister Marvelous had a clever smile across his face. Looking her over, he remembered how she had been practically a kid when he first met her, just a rookie reporter back then. But she was very clearly not a child anymore.

"The funeral, y'know. It was so sad." Her face became droopy as she demonstrated how torn up she was inside over it all.

Still hovering nearby, Dave realized he had not taken a breath in several moments. It felt so surreal to be there in the same room with his childhood idol. Looking him up and down, he could see the classic lines of a warrior. The suit had evolved over the years, and the man within had aged, but it was still Mister Marvelous, in the flesh. *Wow!*

But as he watched them chit-chat, he noticed the shocks of gray in Marv's hair. His suit was woven from top quality Duranium fibers, with alloy armoring in all of the critical places. Built by a genius, the suit had kept the man alive on so many missions. Dave's eyes slowly took it in as he noticed the scuffs in the back of the suit where it was worn from use.

There was also a slouch to Marv's posture. No longer the twenty-something alpha-male, he was closer to grandpa than hunk. Still, he seemed to be in good condition, for a man of his vintage. Far from his former glory, it was clear that the hero had seen better days.

"So what're YOU doing out here?" This time it was Polly's turn to flip the question. It was a valid point; Mister Marvelous' territory was clear across the galaxy. *This was Captain Collider territory.*

"Well, I need to do some investigative research on Ming, so I thought I'd ninja in here, hitch a ride on your shuttle so I'm invisible to their sensors, and detach right before you enter the docking bay. Then I go do my secret hero-recon mission. You know; usual stuff." Smiling, could still lay on the smolder. Having been a dashing and daring public figure for more than 30 years now, Mister Marvelous still knew how to earn his nickname.

Giving him a wary eye, Polly was visibly skeptical.

"Don't worry," He promised her. "You two will have complete deniability in this. There's no way you could be expected to know there's a guy wearing a proton suit attached to your hull. After that I do my *thang*, then zip out of there unnoticed. Eazy-peazy." Again he flashed a smile as a lock of hair fell down over his forehead.

Dave could not help but be mesmerized

by the way that Marvelous seemed so cavalier about it all. He was talking about penetrating the most deadly ship in the galaxy, getting past 10,000 soldiers, 20,000 killer-death-drones, and defeat a security network so big that it had its own zip-code. All of this, by himself, with nothing more than the weapons he carried or captured. *No pressure, right?*

"So, how have you been?" Giving a smile as he loomed over her, Marv flicked his eyes towards the back of the ship.

"I've been okay." Although she spoke in a happy tone, her eyes took on an edge as the super hero edged closer.

From his vantage behind the two, Dave got the impression that Marvelous was simply hitting on the buxom reporter. It surprised him little to see her scowl at the man. After all, she was currently dating Captain Legend. What would she want with a has-been Super who was old enough to be her father?

Remaining polite, Polly knew exactly how to escape from the aging hero.

"Oh, I need to go to the little reporter's room." She interjected between smiles, her lips a tad pouty. Turning to Dave she looked so sincere. "Do we have time before we dock…for me to freshen up?"

"Oh, yeah, yeah." Dave nodded like a bobblehead. "Plenty of time. We won't even get to the outer sensors for like ten minutes."

"M'lady." Stepping back, Marvelous was gracious as he let her past in the narrow walkway. Waiting until she was out of the room, Mister Marvelous suddenly turned his attention to the cameraman.

"So, kid…?" Tossing his gloves onto the dashboard, Marv flopped down into the copilot's chair.

"Dave. Dave Meadows." He stammered out loud.

"Glad to meet ya, kid…" Shaking his hand, Marvelous flashed his best smile before he pretended to think of something. "Say, aren't you Jenna Meadows' son?"

Dave was shocked that the man knew anything at all about him.

"You know my Mom?" Breathless, the cameraman was dying to know how.

"Oh, she was on the school board back on Darnum. My daughter went to school at Excelsior High." He beamed as he referred to the elite school.

"I went to Bleakum." Dave's voice

dropped an octave as he thought of those dark and musty hallways. Something else occurred to him. "I didn't know you had a daughter?"

Mister Marvelous seemed to pause at that, as if he realized he had said too much. His smile flickered a bit before he took another path. "She died. Fifteen years ago; cosmic explosion at the academy."

Dave remembered the story well. Having been ten years old the year it happened, it had been something every kid in town knew about. An unexplained cosmic explosion had...*obliterated* five girls. That had been the way the press had described it. Whatever it was that had done the job, it not only killed the students, but reduced them to nothing more than little piles of dust. The story had been on every screen on the planet for a year straight. The top 5 students in the school, all besties, vaporized during debate class. There was even a made-for-TV miniseries that chronicled the event.

"Oh, dude, I'm so sorry." Although Dave did truly feel sad for the man, in the back of his fan-boy mind he was connecting the details when something occurred to him. "Is that why you killed Oligarch and Slavel?

Because they used red energy like was used at the academy?"

For Dave it was a true epiphany. All these years, he and the rest of the galaxy all thought the battle was over humanitarian issues. But now he knew that both of those epic confrontations were fueled by revenge. That explained why Marv did not arrest them, or turn them over to the local forces like he usually did. Everyone had thought he killed them in such deliberate fashion just to let people know that this Superhero stuff was for real. At the time there had been cries of fakery among some of the ranks. But after Captain Marvel used his Mark XXI enhanced armor-suit to rip those villains in half with his bare hands, there was no further dispute.

"Keep that to yourself, kid." Something in his look said he did not regret those actions.

"Anyhow, how're things going with your boss, Pollyanna?" Flicking his head back towards the powder room, the superhero had a clever smile on his face.

"She's a boss." He shrugged, not taking the bait. "She's not as nice as she looks."

"Awwww, you just haven't known her long enough." Marv brushed back a lock of his hair. Really it was just acting; his hair was held in place with an intrinsic field. *A hero is only as good as his best profile shot.*

"You've known her a long time?" That interested the cameraman.

"Yeah, you could say that I helped her become what she is now. I was her first interview when she was a new reporter…must have been ten…twelve years?" He thought about it before offering a new estimate. "It was right after the second battle of *Moleki*, so that woulda been eleven years ago. Yep, she was this pretty little *thang*, just bursting with some really great questions. She had a lead on a Caluim ring, and she suspected they were part of Gort's network. So I took the tip, busted some heads, and did eventually track down that fat bastard Gort and put an end to him. After that we used to help each other out that way; she had leads that I turned into arrests, and we both got front page exposure. You can't buy publicity like that."

Dave seemed taken aback by the shallowness of that last statement. Not saying anything, he simply showed a disappointed look on his face. From his seat, Marv could see it right away.

"Don't give me that look, kid. I'm not

crazy about all the press either. It makes my personal life a complete mess, but there are some harsh realities to this superhero gig. For one, it doesn't pay the bills."

"I read that Captain Coal makes six figures…?" Cocking his head to one side, this was an element of their lives that he knew very little about.

Marvelous just chuckled at the mention of that name. "That guy is a corporate hero; of course they pay him well. Those guys are essentially lobbyists with machine guns. Do me a favor and never compare me to one of them guys. Most of them don't even have real powers; they're all suit."

"How do you afford to do it? Rich benefactor, secret government organization?" The cameraman's eyes lit up as he pondered the financial mysteries of a Super.

"Actually I get a modest salary from a GoFundMe account. Most of us legit heroes do. It's not a huge salary or anything, I could have made more money if I went back to selling cars, but it pays the bills so I can focus on stopping evil on a full-time basis." Waving a hand, Marv instinctively sent a link to the account. It was just habit for him; *the account wasn't going to fill itself.*

Grinning like a fan-boy, Dave enjoyed hearing this perspective of the hero world. But even the greatest champion still needs to eat. Duranium battle-armor isn't free. He was just about to gush some more when a question popped into his head.

"What'd you mean when you said guys like Captain Coal were…lobbyists with guns?"

Mister Marvelous furrowed his eyebrows. Decades in front of a mirror had taught him the perfect way to show sincerity. "Y'see, years ago me and the other supers all figured out that if we beat on Ming hard enough, often he'll change the law or practice that we were fighting him for in the first place. It's the strangest thing, but even if you lose, if you can ring his bell a few times real good, a couple of months later, outta the blue, the laws get changed. It's not always a complete victory, usually there's some kind of compromise to it, but the world gets changed. And really, that's why I put on this suit in the first place; to make the galaxy a better place."

"So the corporate heroes are paid to go and fight Ming to get him to change laws in favor of their employers?" There was a tinge of disgust to the cameraman's voice as he made the revelation.

Marv shrugged listlessly before glancing over his shoulder towards the bathroom. "She's been in there a long time. You don't think it's that time…?"

"Naw. Most likely there's just a mirror in there." Dave admitted half-heartedly.

"Ouch! Penis-envy much?" The elder chuckled.

Dave misunderstood the joke at first. "Penis…you don't mean she's a he…?"

"What?! NO!" Marv waved two hands to clear the air. "I was just saying that you seemed jealous…"

"I'm not jealous, she's just…" Dave stopped short before reconsidering his next words. "She's just…difficult sometimes."

"Yeah, you're telling me kid." Marv nodded in agreement. Clearly they had some checkered history together.

Something beeped on the dashboard. Looking up, Dave could see it was the outer marker warning. Just another few hundred thousand kilometers and they would need to enter approach plan Delta. Already the course was laid out on the nav screens.

"And that would be my signal to get in

place before we start running into scanner-bots." Rising up, Marvelous was about to engage his helmet when he paused beside Dave. "Kid, this is nothing personal, but I probably shouldn't have said some of those things, so for the security of the realm, I gotta flash you."

Dave was not sure what that cryptic statement meant. While he was pondering it, Marv engaged his helmet unit, then aimed a fist at the cameraman's face. Holding it just a few feet away, there was a sudden flash of neutronic energy, right in Dave's face.

So although Marv did not actually punch Dave, the energy wave left the younger man stunned in his chair. Known for its ability to purge short-term memories, the neutronic energy blast was typically used to quietly disable sentries and minions. For his own part, the cameraman felt his jaw drop open, tongue fall to one side, drool run out of his mouth and down onto the console. He had absolutely no control over his bodily functions, and all muscles had gone limp. But oddly, he was still conscious. That last detail was not supposed to happen with a neutronic blast; *he should be out cold*. Not only that, but he also should have forgotten their entire conversation. *Perhaps the blast had been delivered wrong?* No, that couldn't be it; the neutronic cannon was one of Mister Marvelous' oldest gimmicks. He had been famous for using that weapon ever since it showed up on the MARK II suits. If anything, Marv was one of the foremost experts in the use of neutronic energy. He had literally written the book on it. *Dave even had a copy.* [Be the Life of the Party with Neutronic Energy by M. Marvelous. Available on Amazon Galactic $6.99 Penguin Press]

By the time Dave could control his muscles enough to sit up, Marvelous was gone out the airlock, and Polly was finally emerging from the restroom. Still a little woozy, he swayed in his seat.

"Oh, did Marv leave?" She pretended to be surprised even though the restroom was right next to the airlock. She would have felt the rotating unit as it locked into battery; there was an unmistakable *thump* that resonated through the floor of the shuttle when the airlock cycled.

"STELLA!" The shout that spilled from his mouth made absolutely no sense he worked to regain control of his face muscles.

"Have you been drinking?" She looked at his drooping lip, then at the drool on the dashboard before snapping her fingers near his head. *"Wakie-wakie, eggs & bakey.* We have an interview with Ming in an hour. You better not screw this up or I will make you walk home. And I am not being metaphorical when I say that; I will fire you, then kick you out the nearest airlock and let you fly home on thrusters. Are…*we*…understanding each other?"

"I like green eggs and ham." A blob of spit dripped out his mouth as he tried to tell her that Mister Marvelous had used his neutronic cannon on him in an attempt to wipe his memory. But try as he may, nothing but useless drivel came out. "daed si luaP!"

"And change your pants before we dock." She looked down at his crotch.

Wet from the release of fluids during his complete loss of muscle control, he suddenly realized he had peed himself.

"Muchos tacos con queso!" He uttered in surprise, both at the wet pants, and at the odd word combinations that spilled out of his maw. He could still feel a little of the blue energy tingling at the base of his skull.

"Have engineering disinfect that chair, then have it thrown it into the nearest star." Her eyes said she was serious.

"Flunk me!" He muttered, relieved that he was at least getting closer to speaking English again.

Their schedule that afternoon had been tight, but there was one thing that Dave had to check on before it distracted him anymore. Pretending to be busy setting up a camera, he dialed the top number on his speed-dial list. Waiting for her to answer, he spoke sub-vocally.

"Mom?" His words told her who it was.

"Oh, David. How is the job? I was watching the news on channel forty-nine and…"

"Mom, how do you know Mister Marvelous?" It was the first question on a very long list of things he wanted to ask her.

There was utter silence on the line for the longest time. Finally breaking the fast, Dave spoke up again. "Mom?"

"I-wa—going-school—academy, going-thru-tunnel-losing you, honey…" Then abruptly the line went dead.

Sitting up, the cameraman knew she was covering up something; he had called the home phone, not her cell phone. So unless she took the entire house out for a drive through a tunnel, it was a safe bet she was lying. Somehow that felt like a hard blow to the young man. In his life he had met a lot of disingenuous people, but the one person in the entire universe who had always spoken the truth was his mother. Dad was never a thing, and no siblings, so essentially the rest of the galaxy was scum by his accounting. But to learn there could be a blemish on his mother's honor…now that bothered him. Truthfully, it felt a little sacrilegious to even think she was in some way bad or amoral.

Surely there was a good explanation. *He just wasn't going to get it from her right now.*

Polly had been in *Diva-mode* since they landed. Her fuse had been shorter than a hand grenade and her specifications for the production were insane. Normally they were rigged for 2 fixed cameras and a 3rd mobile unit. But not today; she wanted 4 fixed cameras, and two mobile, and they all had to be VR rated. Her assertion had been that the network wanted to explore some alternate marketing techniques, but she refused to elaborate on any specifics. Assuming the footage would end up in a video game or maybe a Christmas special, Dave complied. *After all, it wasn't like he had to pay for all the equipment.*

Using a finger to flick the last of the cameras, he had chosen to add a 7th camera, perched at the top of the room for that eagle-eye view. He planned to hold the footage in reserve in case Polly nagged him. Then he imagined how he would suddenly pull out the extra footage and shove it in her face to prove how he had exceeded her specs. Really, it was just his passive/aggressive way to poke his boss in the eye without getting fired in the process.

Wearing all white, Polly's shirt and pant outfit had been digitally printed to very exacting specifications. With the fabric highlighting every curve, and her golden locks flowing down to her shoulders, Polly positively glowed as she exited her dressing room. Standing across the chamber from from Ming and Lotus, she pretended to be oblivious to their gawking.

Even the Morganeese guards were staring

at Polly, but more likely because they thought she looked edible. Virgins on a stick were a popular snack in the BelNar system.

"It's like Jello, on springs." Ming uttered the words hypnotically as he watched her stride across the room.

"Hamina, hamina, hamina." Lotus uttered the words as if he were under a spell. Leering openly, the chief minion twirled a long strand of his greasy wig.

"Hubba hubba." Dave offered his own comment only to be met by vehement stares.

"Cad." Ming sneered.

"Misogynist!' Lotus echoed the sentiment.

"Who are you to be speaking in such derogatory manner about a true lady?" Flexing his bony hands, the dictator showed off his razor sharp nails. According to rumor, he had killed several heroes with nothing more than those fingernails.

"Such a derogatory manner." Lotus echoed his boss's words.

"Perhaps some therapy in one of the pain chambers after work tonight?" Ming pretended as if he were mulling over the idea.

"Please no, I already live in D-block, and they beat me and hit me all damned night.

Isn't that torture enough?" His voice begging as much as it was resigned, Dave simply wanted to get through the day without being spaced.

"D-block?" Ming did a lousy job of concealing his smile as he turned to Lotus. "Did you really billet him with the Morganeese?"

There was the barest hint of a grin from the dictator as he looked down on his chief minion. Waiting for Lotus to nod his greasy head, he finally broke into an open smile.

"That is a truly despotic thing to do to another human being. Simply revolting and cruel on a scale that approaches sociopathic pettiness. I'm so proud of you, son." Chuckling openly, he wrapped his arms around the little minion.

"Thanks, Dad. I tried to put him in steerage, but *she* objected." Gesturing towards Polly, he was soaking up the rare praise.

"Steerage?" Stepping back, Ming held his son by the shoulders. "I remember being thrown into steerage when I was a young minion. I lost my thyroid there. Mmmm. Good times."

"I know; seems like just yesterday that I

was climbing out of the cloning tank for the first time." Lotus had a fond look on his face.

"Oh my," Ming held a hand to his chest in surprise. "And how many has it been now? Ten?"

"Twelve. Twelve times I was killed and restored from the clone bank." Smiling, Lotus's happy face took an odd lilt as he completed the statement. "This year."

Ming sighed as he thought of all the times it had happened. "Well, luckily you're fully insured."

At opposite ends of the room, the journalists eyed the duo. In his own mind Dave was wondering why Ming and Lotus looked so dissimilar if one was a clone of the other. Or was Lotus a clone of the son who was lost or killed? And if that was the case, who was Mom? *Medusa?* Knowing the villainy before him, he could scarcely imagine what happened in the privacy of Ming's bedroom. Dave envisioned a room filled with whips and torture devices, and constant porn running on 37 massive screens around the room. Thinking better about it, he realized he was just being biased and projecting his own tastes onto Ming.

On the surface Polly was pleasant and

agreeable. But really she wanted to get this interview started before something bad happened. She had been feeling it coming on all day, and hoped it would wait just another hour. *Oh, if only there was a pill so you didn't have to have a period every five years*, she had posted her dilemma on social media just an hour before. Holding a hand over her stomach, she telegraphed her discomfort despite her best acting. Finally her eyes narrowed to slits as she shot Dave a look of death. Snapping to action, the photojournalist knew he'd better start the interview before he found himself on a donor list. She had been pretty caustic lately.

"Uh, let's go ahead and get started, if that is okay with your imperious-ness, sir?" Dave tried to backpedal at the end.

"Yes, lets. I have a colony to obliterate at three." Nodding agreeably, the Emperor moved over and seated his flowing robes in the bigger of the two chairs.

"But sir, they insisted that the check was in the mail." Lotus whispered to his father.

"Bah." Holding up a fist, he quashed the discussion. "Poverty is no excuse for not paying your luxury taxes!"

With a writing tablet in hand, Polly tried

to look thoughtful as she posed her first question.

"The council of Ives has just ruled that…" Her face blanched slightly, leaving only the red rouge on her cheeks for color. "I…need to…private things…"

Gesturing back towards her dressing room, she was up out of her chair in a flash and high-stepping it all the way to there. Two seconds after the door slammed shut, Lotus broke the silence.

"Told you it was menstrual." Holding out a bony hand, the minion had a subtle grin on his face. "Pay up."

"Oh!" Shaking his head, Ming seemed bewildered by it. "I was sure she had been taken over by Zombie worms and was being manipulated towards their evil purpose. She had all the symptoms."

"It's just her period. She announced it on SelfGlorify.com two hours ago." Dave thought nothing of revealing that detail. Especially since it was trending like crazy on twitter.

"Infidel, cad. To speak of her in such…?" In his anger, Ming skipped definition and moved straight to the penalty phase. "To the torture chambers for him. Two hours. That should be the attitude adjustment that your Hank Williams sang of so eloquently. Take him away."

Waving his fingers as if he were brushing something away, the dictator's order was immediately carried out as guards grabbed each of Dave's arms.

"Turn the pain setting up to eleven." Lotus added with a sneer.

The cameraman was breathless as he was lifted up off the ground. He had heard the legend of Ming's torture booths. Everybody else's booths only went up to ten. But Ming's went all the way to eleven; the extra detent was saved for the most loathsome of offenders and salesmen. The idea scared him so much that he feared peeing his pants right there in the throne room.

"Wait, I..." his pleas were swallowed up as the far wall was vaporized in a cloud of dust and debris. He felt something hit his head, and then realized that it was actually his head hitting the ground. Not only that, he was upside down.

As the explosion still echoed through the chamber, sharp daggers shot out of the dust cloud, several passing just inches from Dave's head. He could hear the blades sink into the guard's flesh, followed by big splashes of blood on the floor as their carotids were severed. Within seconds the guards fell to the ground, choking on their own blood.

Free now, the cameraman scuttled backwards behind a desk as he saw something begin to emerge from the cloud of dust. He was almost safe when someone shoved him. Looking over he was surprised to see Lotus, sans his greasy black wig, hunkered down under the desk.

"Find your own hiding place!" He hissed before kicking Dave in the face. "I'm not going to be the thirteenth clone to crawl out of that damned cloning tank. That bitch be crazy!"

Crawling as fast as he could through the metal and debris, Dave made the mistake of sparing a look at whatever was now floating in the gaping hole in the doorway. There, clad in black latex that looked as if it had been applied with an airbrush, was *Wanda B. Wicked*, mistress of the dark, slayer of Thanos's brother Tad, and Domina of the Savo Star System. There was no red-blooded male citizen in the galaxy that did not know exactly who Wanda was. *And every one of them knew to run like hell when they saw her.*

Unfortunately, Dave froze when he should have been fleeing. He had heard the rumors of how she recruited her minions, those poor men who were held in cybernetic bondage and forced to do her bidding. In his mind he imagined himself as a drone, with sensors protruding from the leather that would cover his entire face and body. It terrified him to think that he was about to become one of her minion gimps. *Worse yet; they offered no dental plan.*

Aiming a fist at the cameraman, Wanda released a burst of purple energy. Turning away, she did not even wait to see if she hit him. But true to her aim, the plasma collided with the cameraman, immediately burning out the camera he wore. His brain felt as if he were chewing on a tazer. His whole body buzzed and burned. He was sure he was on fire for real.

Wriggling on the ground he realized that it was not all in his head. The blast had indeed set his shirt on fire. *Damned Rayon!* He flipped about trying to get the burning fabric off. Terrified, he realized that even though the fire was hot as hell, he did not see any serious burns. He only hoped he could get to cover before she blasted him again. Usually one shot from Wanda was more than enough to fry a mortal. He was lucky to still be alive. But that concerned him because the only reason she would not kill him outright was if she wanted to toy with him first. *Suddenly he wished the first shot had killed him.*

"Burn worm!" Holding out a fist, this time instead of a single blast, she let loose with a sustained beam that cut the bookshelf he was hiding behind into two neat pieces. Swinging the beam to one side lazily she cut one of the support columns.

Floating a meter off the deck, the dark goddess watched intently as the column toppled over on top of Polly's dressing room. Crashing to pieces, it effectively blocked the door with rubble. No doubt the reporter's ears were ringing after that. Awake or unconscious, one thing was sure; Polly was not coming out of her dressing room any time soon.

Slowly settling to the floor, Wanda strode on stilettos until she was directly over the cameraman. Holding both fists out, she began charging her capacitors for a killing shot. But it was the bejeweled hand on her shoulder that caused the huntress to pause her killing spree. Looking back, she could see Ming shaking his head.

"But my dear, I am just exterminating the vermin." She defended her action, her fists still aimed at Dave's face. "If I saw a rat run across the floor, would you not expect me to eradicate the entire species from all existence? He is vermin."

"He's an intern." Ming gave a shrug as if there were not dead soldiers at every entrance. *"And a legacy."* He lowered his voice for the last part.

"Oh?" Wanda raised one eyebrow in intrigue. "Which one?"

Using his hand, Ming made a flapping motion. There was immediate recognition on her face before it dissolved into a leer. "So this is…"

She was about to say something when Ming squoze her arm. On the ground Dave was just wondering how much longer before he was burned down to a stump. Like anyone who followed the heroes, he knew that the villainess had once used her purple energy beams to cut open a vault door just to steal a prototype suit. Based on sheer wattage, it would only take her a few seconds and to turn him into a puddle of soup.

"Mmmm. Out of professional courtesy I will not burn your brains out of your skull, or turn you into one of my cybernetic gimp drones." She gestured playfully towards her own minion who stood nearby, a briefcase in hand. The gimp's skin had the pallor of someone who had been dead for a week. Her face was essentially one robotic eye, one crazy-eye, and a mouth stitched shut with twine. *But once you got past her shocking face, she had quite the feminine form.*

Although Dave felt glad to be spared, Wanda's gimp-minion winked suggestively at him with her crazy-eye. He was unsure what exactly that meant, but he definitely feared sending the wrong signal.

"Sooo, David Meadows, if you are not gone in ten seconds, I will kill you in the face." Smiling sweetly, Wanda flexed her fist as purple energy seemed to course through her arm.

Scuttling out of there, the cameraman got as far as the main door before he paused to look back. There the minion was laying out the contents of the briefcase.

Standing nearby, Wanda Wicked simply stood hands on hips facing the despot in robes. Pretending as if she were checking her nails, she intentionally ignored the man who stood a few feet away. As the mistress of the darkness, this was but one of her powers. Clearly Ming was intoxicated by her very presence. Buxom and bold, the brunette intended to do things on her own schedule.

Ming's anticipation was thick enough to cut with a knife. His skinny fingers seemed to dance nervously at as he glanced between Wanda and whatever was concealed in the case on the table. Finally after the longest pause, the mistress of the dark reached down and flipped open the suitcase. There for all to see, were dozens of objects of torture and pain. Dave could not even imagine what most were for. He suddenly realized there may be something worse than two hours in the torture tank. Clearly, she had come to do awful things to someone.

Dave realized he had lingered in the doorway just a bit too long when Wanda spotted him there.

"This ain't a peep show, little boy." Her voice was honeysuckle sweet right before it turned sinister. "Now get out while you still have legs to drag yourself."

She turned back to Ming, confident that

the cameraman would get gone as fast as he humanly could. Only a *sick-fuck sociopath* would stick around when Wanda was in one of these moods…and that sociopath's name was Ming.

Dave just started to turn away when he noticed Wanda's from behind. Truly her form was perfection. Despite his fear of being murdered by the arch-villainess, he could not help but notice her graceful curves. His eyes settling on her butt, he could not help but compare it to Polly's equally flawless ass.

That's when he realized something; that really was Polly's ass!

No, can't be, he thought as he scuttled away. Polly is blonde and pure, and Wanda is a brunette with wicked-evil eyes covered by a mask. One was an ace reporter, and the other was an arch-villainess. Aside from being extraordinarily hot, they had nothing in common.

Nope, it's an absurd idea, he thought to himself as he fled that room of pain.

It was over eight hours later when the guards told Dave he could go pick up his gear from the interview. Combing through the debris in the former executive office, he found 6 of the cameras, but they all appeared to be dead. When he tried to connect an umbilical to each, he found that their internals were completely and utterly fried.

"She most likely disrupted the circuits when she used the neutronic blast on me. Such exquisite pain." Ming's voice came from the back corner of the room. Finally sitting up amongst the wreckage, the dictator looked completely out of sorts. Shirtless, his beard frayed, he even had bits of metal shavings stuck to his cheeks. Truly, he looked like someone had blown him up. Despite how out of place he looked, the most atypical thing was the dreamy smile on his face. "Such exquisite pain indeed…"

Like anyone, Dave knew of the use of neutronic energy in the sex industry. The effect was claimed to be better than autoerotic asphyxiation. His mother had warned him against the evils of such things; now as he looked at the charred and seared camera in his hand, he could see she was right.

"Yabba-dabba-doo…" He said in a dry voice before tossing the scorched camera into a bin. Even the memory chips were toast.

Shirtless as he sat up in the rubble, Ming's upper torso was pasty white like the rest of him. Skinny, and showing a few ribs, he looked almost frail. Without the robes, or the tall neck shield he wore, he looked far from the regal imperator of evil that they were all used to seeing.

With a tall cup of steaming coffee in one hand, Dave worked his way over the girders towards Ming. As he moved, the cameraman kept a watchful eye out for his robes.

It took a few seconds before he finally spotted Ming's charred robes under a severed arm. A few feet away were his boots as well. Recovering the items with his free hand, the cameraman was still blowing on his coffee that was *waaaaay* too hot to drink yet. The coffee machine down the hall was an insane device. More than once Dave had kidded that the thing practically dispensed mocha *plasma*, the coffee was so damned hot!

Holding up the clothing, he noticed the tall heels in Ming's boots. The battle-boots would have given the man at least three inches of additional height. Brushing it off, he cautiously made his way toward where the Emperor still sat stunned in the wreckage.

"Here you go…" Dave was just holding up the robes and boots when he felt greedy little hands prying the coffee from his grip. As if he were dying of thirst, Ming had the cup to his lips as he held it with both hands. "Careful, that's really…hot…"

Standing there watching, he witnessed the dictator guzzle the entire cup in one long pull. Smacking his lips, he graciously handed the empty cup back to Dave. "Be sure and see that gets into the proper recycle bin."

"Sure…" Exchanging clothes for the empty cup, Dave kept his opinions to himself. Standing up, Ming wrapped himself in his red armored robe before scooping up his boots. For just a moment there, Dave and he stood facing each other from several feet away. It occurred to the cameraman that without his elevated boots, Ming was roughly the same height as he. Immediately his mind flashed to an image of the bald man from the funeral. *Naw, couldn't be…*

Flopping down in a broken chair, the dictator dumped the plaster dust out of his boot before struggling to force his foot into it.

"Could I ask you a question?" Still holding the empty cup, Dave had finally summed up the courage to ask about something that had been on his mind.

"Technically, you just did. So yes, you may ask me one additional question." As the coffee began to work on the old man, Ming was fast becoming his old self again. Already his voice was taking on its usual shrill tone.

"Is it true that you often change laws as a result of your battles with the supers?" Dave just threw it out there.

The question seemed to surprise Ming as he looked sideways at the young photojournalist.

"What an odd thing to ask." He gave the tiniest of smiles, his eyebrows knit in a sinister look. "But in answer to your specific question, yes, I do frequently alter the progress of galactic advancement after reevaluating the impact it may have on a specific region or star system. That I admit to freely, and I have done so on many occasions."

Nodding sincerely, the dictator felt no remorse for his actions. Really, he acted as if it were simply part of the process.

"Hmmm. Technically, since you are the established ruler of the galaxy, they are terrorists for opposing you in armed conflict, so technically your governing is influenced by terrorists…?" Showing a big, stupid smile, Dave made sure it was obvious that he was kidding.

Chuckling, Ming saw the jab for what it was; a playful jest. Luckily, the imperious leader enjoyed a good verbal bout in the morning. As a man who considered himself the smartest being in the galaxy, Ming felt he should be able to out-spar any opponent.

"Yes, that is one way to look at it. But let me ask you this; what is the difference between one of your elected officials and these beings whose only real sin is being on the wrong side of the law?"

"Uhhhh, well the elected officials are elected. We specifically choose them to represent us. The heroes just…well…they just get powers somehow and start battling you in the name of their local cause. No one elected them…technically. I mean, I'm the last person in the world to bash the supers, I have like…three metric tons of comic books in my room at home. I practically beat-off to superhero comic books, but just to play devil's advocate. Y'know?" Feeling bold, he could see that the dictator was finding amusement in this debate. Ming was usually on the other side of this argument.

"Consider this perspective, young man: these heroes, these men, and women, and hermaphrodites, that put on that battle-armor every day, they are the ones who have risen up from the bovine masses, who have stood apart from all others and proven that they were worthy of being heard. These are the beings that are willing to risk their very existence for a principle, and it is their intestinal fortitude that commands my respect in these things. The rest of society is composed largely of cattle, and should be managed as such. But when the herd is in need, a hero will always rise up amongst them. It is these men and women who truly speak for their people. Not those filthy, lingering politicians who supplicate and plead for their jobs. They are not leaders; a true leader does not beg a people to permit him to rule. No, they take control of their realm and hold it with an iron fist until such a time as they are no longer relevant."

Holding up a bony fist of death, Ming demonstrated how he held the galaxy in his firm grip.

"So what about the corporate heroes? Aren't they just lobbyists with guns?"

The ruler gave that a strange look, as if he had heard the phrase before. Dave wondered briefly if he had said too much. But after a thoughtful pause, the dictator answered with a glint in his eyes.

"Many, many centuries ago there was a great nation known as America. My great-great-great-great-great-great-great…great-grandfather actually came to that great nation to help build a thing called a railroad. It was this curious track made with two metal rails, and a vehicle slid upon it. So barbarically primitive that it absolutely tickles the imagination, no?"

Ming raised an eyebrow as he waited for Dave to agree with him before continuing.

"Anyhoo, at the apex of its power the country survived by a political balance it struck. You see, they had two political groups: the Democraps, and the Repugnicans. Both very powerful groups, they controlled equal parts of the governments. The Democraps were the party of the people, and though well intentioned, they were mollycoddlers. Always enacting laws to protect themselves from pollution and toxic waste, and whining about the environment and the air…   But The

Repugnicans represented industry and big business and conservative ideals. Their ranks included most of the wealthiest in the nation, the ones whose money kept their entire economy afloat. Their companies kept citizens working, paying taxes, and voting Repugnican. Without big business, America would not have been the industrial giant it was, but rather it would have been a smattering of small states with little collective power. But big business gave America power, as well as corporate tendrils all over the planet. So with that in mind I ask you; do those people, the ones whose money keeps our economy afloat, who keep people like you and the lovely Miss Polly employed, should not those people have a voice at the table as well?"

Dave was stuck for an answer. He had to admit, Ming was right. Industry needed to have its concerns included in the governing process. There needed to be a balance between the needs of each group.

"But in answer to the underlying question you were really asking; No, I do not accord the same level of respect to manufactured heroes as I do those who are natural born of their powers. If you have no power without the suit, then you cannot be a true champion. Nonetheless, I enjoy their battles, and take into consideration legislative requests being tabled by their corporations. Since I outlawed political donations twenty years ago, these companies need to spend their lobbying budgets somewhere. Some men play golf, I like to beat down young upstarts."

Holding up a finger, Ming showed a true smile as if he were examining a fond memory.

"So, did you know that Captain Legend escaped at the last second?" Dave figured he would keep asking questions as long as the old guy was feeling chatty. He may never get an opportunity like this again.

Ming gave the young man a stern look before asking a simple question. "Is this off the record?"

"Uh…yeah. Totally. Your girlfriend completely fried all the cameras." Dave showed the last of the ground cameras. The battery packs had all blown out the side.

Leaning forward, Ming's voice had a hushed tone to it.

"You see, back in the early days of my reign, there were hundreds of these supers, rising up here and there. It seemed like there was always some new kid in town who wanted to challenge the fastest gun in the west. We would battle, and I would smite them. Sometimes they would limp away, sometimes they were swept up with a broom and carried away." The old man paused for Dave to laugh at his joke.

"But with time I realized that these heroes were finite, and their numbers were declining due to death, dismemberment, retirement, maternity leave, or simply because they were growing old. It became evident that if I continued to be wasteful, then very soon there would be none left. To cause the extinction of valor would be every bit as bad as causing the extinction of an animal species. By my standards, both are equally amoral acts." Nodding solemnly, he remembered those early battles.

"Didn't you obliterate planet MinKusk? There were like...fifteen million different biological species on that planet." Dave held his breath, hoping he had not gone too far.

Instead Ming merely shrugged. "Twas closer to twenty million species, and they were all safely transferred to ParaLara in the Deng system. The creatures don't even know they're not on MinKusk anymore."

Dave's mouth sputtered as if the computer in his brain had experienced a syntax error.

"Blu-but…what? Where? You made a backup of a whole planet?" The cameraman was in awe of what he had just heard.

Ming shifted his position so he faced the cameraman. Giving a grimace, he held up his knuckles.

"My apologies, young man. I should not have mentioned that last bit. It's quite classified. Let's just back up to the part where we were talking about corporate heroes." And with that Ming's fist flashed a blue ball of energy at the young cameraman.

"Oowwwww!" Dave gave out a cry as the energy pained him briefly. "Please don't do that." He begged Ming. This was the second time that day that someone had tried to wipe his memory.

Ming observed the photojournalist's diminished reaction to his energy blast before muttering a deep *Hmmm.*

Blinking away the spots in his eyes, Dave took a cautious step back. "Y'know, I gotta get some rack time while the soldiers are out on drill, otherwise I'll have to sleep in the boiler room again…I'll just let you and Lotus get on with your day.

Turning his head left and right, he realized that the greasy-haired minion was nowhere in sight. It was odd for Ming to be seen without his chief lackey in tow.

"Where is that guy, anyhow?"

Ming raised his eyebrows before replying. "Oh, he is under that girder just behind you."

Dave jumped straight up into the air at the sight of Lotus's contorted face staring at him from under twisted wreckage. It was obvious that his death had been painful indeed.

"Oh shit!" Dave tripped over debris trying to retreat from the corpse. "Dood, I am soooo sorry, your son…?"

"Oh," Ming shrugged it off. "Lotus is in the bio-oven right now. He should be ready for duty by dinner time. His matrix is backed up live-stream to the ship's mainframe, so he doesn't lose a second of his previous life."

"Cool." Dave initially thought it sounded awesome, and then thought better of it. "You mean it backs up everything, even…" He pantomimed Lotus being crushed by the girder, accented by gurgling sounds.

"Even that." Nodding, Ming agreed. "Your death is a very personal and philosophical event in your life. To take that from him would be stealing key developmental components to his sociological development as a minion. We arch-villains are forged in the hottest of ovens. This is perfectly healthy for him to experience."

"Nine out of ten therapists would probably disagree, but sure." Dave gave an awkward laugh as he turned his head. He had been slowly becoming aware of a thumping sound. He had thought it was just the engines spooling up, but this was not the constant tick-tick-tick of the Stratex TransLuminal reactors. Really it was more of a random clanging, muffled by walls. Turning to walk towards a spot where the metal and faux-stone were piled up high he could just detect the intermittent clanging every few seconds. There was a guard posted a few feet away, staring off into space.

"Do you hear that?" He asked the soldier.

"Yep. Sum zed's klangin' wit a wrench or sumtin." Shrugging it off, the beast seemed to find it immaterial to their duties.

"How long they been banging?" Dave kept his voice level. He did not want to pick a fight with someone from D-block. *He'd be ShekNar'd every night.*

"A while, I guesses. Since I come on

shift, mebbe?" Again the armored pile of tumors confirmed the facts.

"So someone has been in there all night, banging away trying to summon help, and you didn't say anything?" His tone went up an octave; he was irked. Especially since he remembered whose dressing room that was.

"My job be to guard and kill. None needed either. No one told me to say nuthin 'bout some trapped *hey-u-man*. That not my department." The soldier simply could not understand the problem.

Shaking it off, Dave swallowed his anger. Really, he just wanted to save his job without incurring the wrath of any of his bunk-mates. Besides, he needed the brute's help right now.

"Help me get this stuff out of the way of the door." Pointing to the girder that weighed at least a metric ton, Dave expected the soldier to summon assistance. Instead the beast simply grabbed the metal in a bear-hug, and wretched it free with enough force to send bolts flying. After that brutal move, he very gingerly set it down in a corner.

Opening the door, he was greeted by Polly as she stumbled out in a stench. Immediately, the cameraman recoiled at the noxious smell.

"Oh mein gott in himmel!" Dave called out as he stepped back. "You smell like ass! No, no, you smell like Satan ate Louisiana chili, with extra-extra jalapenos, then he shit that into a bucket, and they fermented that into a wine…that's what you smell like. Holy shite!"

"It's the dressing room!" Polly burst out on the verge of tears. "The explosion caused the toilet to burst, and I have been trapped in a sealed box of human guano." Flexing her fist, she tried to convey to her employee just how close to snapping she was. "I have been in there for days…**days!**" She grabbed him by the collar and shouted into his face.

"It was more like eight hours." Dave kept his voice soft; he knew better than to jostle nitroglycerin.

"YOU LEFT ME!" Her voice faded to a breathless wisp at the end before she sagged against a wall.

Dave rushed to catch her, but she shoved him away. Turning to cast a hateful look, first at Dave, then Ming, she finally turned away and began walking towards her quarters.

"If anyone needs me, I will be

unavailable. Unless your name is *Room Service*, don't call or knock for the next three days." Tripping over a broken heel, she looked terrible, with grime and unmentionables smeared all over her pretty white outfit. Even her blonde curls had not escaped the shit-shower that was her dressing room.

Dave stood looking at the brown splashes that coated the walls of her dressing room before giving a whistle in surprise. *When that septic line had ruptured, it must have been like a brown geyser in there.*

But at least he wasn't fired.

Back in his room, Dave sat toying with the camera interface in his mind's eye. The software was actually a cutting board that allowed him to edit the footage they had taken thus far on their year-long project to document Ming. There was tons of film in there, much of it still waiting to be tagged and edited down to the interesting stuff. But in the meantime, he was just about to shut it all down and get some sleep when he noticed that one of the camera icons was listed as still being active. Right away he was wide awake.

"You're kidding me…" He was breathless to see that the ceiling camera had survived the neutronic blast. It made sense really; the unit had been parked high in the rafters and safe from Wanda's sexual energy blasts. Not only was it still working, but it had been recording live-feed for hours.

Tapping at time index 22:13, he found the exact spot where he himself had scampered out of the chamber, under threat of death. He watched with fascination as Wanda dragged Ming around in a most humbling way. Then came the beatings, and the electrocutions, and the plasma blasts.

Dave hit the FFW button three times to be sure he skipped well past that part. Never a fan of the whole S&M scene, he really had no appetite for it.

After hours of torture and abuse, *specifically Wanda torturing and abusing Ming*, their time together ended with a massive burst of energy that burnt out every circuit for five meters. Floating away on a black cloud of smoke, Miss Wicked made her exit, leaving the old man stunned in the debris where Dave had found him.

Fast forwarding, he got to watch his own conversation with the ruler, followed by

Polly's release from the shite-box. Stopping and zooming in several times, he had to admit that even dipped in shit, she was still hotter than the sun. He had to take a deep breath as he appreciated the 3d view straight down her top.

"Now that's a scenic view. They should designate that a national monument." He cackled to himself before she walked out of camera view. Irritated, he tried to backup the video to that spot. But instead, he hit the wrong control and switched the view to real-time. Suddenly he was watching Ming shuffle across the floor of his office while dozens of janitor bots worked to clean up the mess. It was something that happened enough that the ship's crew had a whole process worked out. Dave was just about to switch back to the twin vistas of Polly's pure heart when something blocked the camera for a moment.

Blinking, Dave initially thought it was a cleaner bot, but that theory changed when he saw the thing suspend itself from a rope before slowly dropping down like a spider. Lower and lower it slunk on a single strand of rope, until finally it grabbed the dictator.

Gripping him tightly, the spider zipped

back up the line far enough to yank Ming off the ground. There was a loud shout that sounded a lot like BOOO. Immediately Ming's legs jumped as if he had been completely surprised by the event.

But it was the laughter that caught Dave's attention. He knew the sound of Mister Marvelous anywhere. The hero found it hilarious that he had surprised the evil overlord. Another split second of laughing and he dropped Ming to the ground unceremoniously.

"Clark! You scared the shit out of me!" Ming pretended to clasp a hand over his heart as if it were frail.

Dropping to the ground, Mister Marvelous gave a wave of his hand before his repelling rope automatically recovered itself to his accessory belt. Laughing so hard he could barely walk straight, the hero would stop every few feet to imitate Ming's surprised expression before bursting out in yet more laughter. Each time he found it funnier than the last.

Although it took a few seconds, Ming's scowl slowly turned to a laugh as he realized that it was indeed a truly epic move. It was the kind of class-act that only the old-timers could pull off. *The new generation of heroes were all about flashes and flames, but none of the subtleties.*

"You can laugh now, but you should know that Loki is in charge of the Karma department, and I hear he has a real sense of humor. You never know when he will swap out your shampoo with Nair." Giggling, Ming picked himself up off the floor. "Beer?"

"Hell yeah!" Marv agreed readily as a bot dragged a padded chair over for him to use. "I gotta get my fluids back up. I'm dehydrated from that little minion of Wanda's. She may not look like much in all that leather, with the bloody stitches holding her mouth shut and all, but once you get her out of that suit, she's a stone-cold freak. And I mean stone-cold. She's actually a zombie, so her body temperature is…like room temperature…."

Marv trailed off in his thinking as he accepted a cold one from his foe. Flopping down into a chair across from him, Ming let out a long sigh.

"I'm feeling you, man." Ming's voice seemed to lose its egalitarian tone. "I just ran the Indy 500 with her boss. My, oh, my, is that woman a stickler for accuracy."

The old man had a faraway look in his eyes as he almost shuddered at the remembrance.

"Such a stick-ler…" He muttered to no one.

"Harv, you nail that chick yet?" Mister Marvelous changed the subject slightly. His tone said that this question had come up before.

"Well, not yet…" Ming was aghast at that. "I am not yet worthy; I am still evolving and becoming a better servant. But in time I will ascend to worthiness and she will reward me with blissful…"

"She ain't giving you none." Marv dismissed his explanation.

"I value our relationship; it has helped me grow as a person." Serene in his statement, Ming felt at peace.

Marv watched a cleaning bot dragging a broken riding quip. "Yes, I can see true personal growth."

"Wha's zat?" Ming glanced up as if had missed something.

"Nothing." Marv shrugged it off before putting his feet up on a cleaning bot. Obediently the device shut down and remained there as a foot stool. Behind them a door in the wall opened and another bot was released to make up the workload.

"Well, I had the finance committee look at your proposal for opening up the Klegor mining region, and they say that it could offer a significant revenue potential to the kingdom." All business now, Ming stopped short.

"But the numbers are there. You let those people expand into that region with the tax reduction, call it a tax incentive, and they will open up that whole region and bring in ten times more money than you are going to get from squeezing the farmers on Colbask. Farmers got no money." Gesturing with his beer bottle, Marv knew that he was right. His own people had already studied those same figures.

"Twenty-five percent industrial, fifteen percent personal." The ruler offered tax terms.

"Fifteen percent industrial, with a ten year review, and ten percent personal." Marv raised his eyebrows before continuing. "I got sneakies this time, them's the rules. Ya gotta give it to me or I show everyone your pants-shitting picture."

Waving his hand, Marv had the nearby imager render a picture of Ming screaming as he was hoisted into the air. Slowly the video cycled through images of the dictator at the moment he thought he was about to die in a silk coffin.

"Bah! That's a magnificent loss of revenue up-front. I am afraid I am going to need more." Folding his arms, Ming sat firm before snickering at one of the pictures. "That one is quite funny, the way my tongue is sticking out, and my eyes are all *ahhhh*. You should facebook that one."

Again there was silence as they each waited for the other to break first. Pulling a nail file from his sleeve, Ming kept himself busy sharpening his nails.

"Fine. We battle on your channel, live, primetime, and you win." Marv used his finger to make a dot-dot-dot in the air. "But this time I don't just wanna draw some blood, I want you in the hospital, like with galactic alerts for prayers for the great and powerful Oz who is on his deathbed and may die, but then miraculously, and by means of cybernetic implants, is able to return to public service, though swayed by the emotional trauma of our battle. Ten minutes later they pass the legislation. *Ba-da-bing."*

Rubbing his goatee, the dictator contemplated this scenario. Nodding gently he seemed to like the idea.

"This is some very good writing, I have to admit. I like the entire character arc, the gut-wrenching question; will I survive, will I come back as a brain in a bottle, will I die? Tune in next week and find out…" Chuckling, his eyes gleamed. Something occurred to him. "But I fear this issue is not a big enough draw for primetime. It would seem that if we are going so far as to fake my near-death, then we should have a more epic battle. A broader range of issues would bring in a wider viewer base."

"You could clear more legislation, a lot more." Marv offered. Really it was practical. "Y'know, Captain Proton has been wanting to team up for a few years now, and I have always respected his work, it seems like a good time to have a tag-team fight."

"I was thinking the same." Ming was pleased they were thinking along the same lines. "But I had imagined you and Omega Girl as a team. She could bring in her younger viewers, and you could bring in your…*elderly viewers*, it would play so well."

"Why not Omega Woman?" Marv asked.

Ming completely broke character as he replied in a high pitched voice.

"Have you seen dat ass of hers? That shit's got its own zip code." The dictator was emphatic.

"Oh, that's harsh." Marv tried to dismiss it.

"No, really, I saw her at the grocery store the other day, and from behind I thought she was Beast Girl. Really, look." Waving a finger, Ming shared a photo from his optical implant.

"Ooh!" Marv half stood up before furiously swiping at something in the air. "Delete, delete, delete. Dood, don't send me stuff like that. Those Thorian dick-picks were bad enough, but that should be criminal. I should report you to the authorities."

"I am the authorities." In his chair, Ming gave a coy smile. It pleased him to be able to shock the man still. After a moment the dictator spoke. "You *knowwww*, just spit-balling here, but there is nothing that says we can't have both; Omega girl, **and** Captain Proton." Ming left it open for discussion.

"The Purple Plasma is looking to retire,

he was hoping for one last fight. You could mortally wound him, and he'd retire to Bestos. He's got a boat out there." Nodding Marv could already see the quartet battling evil together. They would contrast each other nicely.

"Oh, the Purple Plasma, I always wanted to battle him. His outfit is totally dope. I always liked his style, always so cool that one was." Smiling, Ming took a swig of the beer in his hand. "His people have several bills pending consideration."

Dave sat back as the footage ran. He was shocked at the degree to which they planned out these battles. But then he had always wondered how they seemed to occur in some place where there were few people to be injured, and plenty of cameras. He had to admit that more once over the years he had thought the timing and placement of these confrontations were a bit too convenient. In the end he had always just assumed that the heroes themselves planned it that way, to maximize coverage. After all, they did survive on public contributions, so broadcasting their work was a smart thing to do. *Even supers gotta eat, right?*

But to see that even the outcome was being arranged, it all began to feel like professional wrestling. *Had it ever been real?*

But he remembered all the times that people had been killed. He himself had covered half a dozen funerals for both sides. Even heroes got killed sooner or later. You could not cheat the reaper forever. Had he not just mourned the loss of Captain Chaos? Surely those funerals were not faked?

Sitting back, it occurred to Dave that he was facing 3 days off. Polly had made it clear that she would not need his services until then…maybe more. After all, the woman was the epitome of a Diva. It could be as much as a week before she returned to work.

"I think it's time for me to use these credentials to find out some answers of my own." Fingering the chip in his wrist, he knew that his Empire security pass would let him access places that he could not have gone if he were still with the network. In fact, he had not yet found a door that his credentials didn't open. Need a space ship? Just use the sign-up sheet in the hanger. For all he knew, he had access to the armory as well. He had never asked, sure that it was a trap to test his loyalty. He had no desire to get caught up in something like that. *Especially after Ming explained the two types of people on his Battle Cruiser.*

No, he'd take a ship, and maybe just **ask** about the armory someday. Right now what he really needed was a trip to the kitchen to pick up a few days worth of supplies. He knew from experience that the guards were lousy about restocking the ships in the hangar, and he was flying all the way to....

Home

Although he pretended to fret about where to begin his investigation, there was never really any dispute where he would go first. Dave was a mamma's boy, and like the dutiful son, he headed straight home.

He had tried to jingle her twice but her line said she was in meetings all day. It occurred to him that she would be able to tell by the metadata on the call that he was getting closer and closer to home.

So it was no surprise she was not at the townhouse when he arrived. She worked out of her office on the backside of the house, and logically that would be where her meetings would be, but the office was dark.

By this point Dave was concerned. His mother had made overt attempts to dodge him ever since he asked about Mister Marvelous. Having known the woman his whole life, he had never known her to lie. By everything he knew; his mother was the paradigm of virtue. Still, something was up.

Sure that she must have a photo or memento stashed somewhere that would explain the whole thing, he began digging through her drawers and closet. An hour and a half later he had done nothing but make a mess. He had been through every shelf, every drawer, and found nothing. *Well, every drawer except the one with his mother's unmentionables in it.* Under no conditions would he insert his hand into that drawer of cotton undies and other mysterious undergarments. From where he stood he could see clearly see a thong that looked to be as wide as one of his shirts. *Yes, the lady had some girth to her these days.*

He was just about to leave around when something occurred to him.

"If I was Mom, and I really wanted to hide something, I'd put it in the one place I programmed my son to never go." He said in a dour voice.

Closing his eyes and taking a deep breath, he reached into her underwear drawer as if it were a hazmat zone. Feeling around he expected to find a photo album, or maybe a diary, but all he found was -CLICK-.

He wasn't sure what it was, so he pressed it again. Still curious, he pressed it four more times quickly.

He could feel a curious sensation from the hairs on the back of his neck, as if a hidden foe was creeping up on him and he could feel their cold breath on the nap of his neck…

Spinning around he saw nothing there. Feeling stupid, he went back to the thing in the drawer. He clicked it, then he clicked it again. Then finally in frustration he clicked it three times quickly before slamming the drawer shut.

"Now I need to decontaminate my arm." He held up his hand as if it were covered in cooties. Rising up, he turned towards the bathroom when something seemed out of place. Pausing, he slowly turned back to the closet as he realized the wall that had been there before was now gone. In its place was a brightly lit display case containing the most petite set of battle armor he had ever seen. Sporting a black-feather paint job, it was a frightening bit of tech. He could see particle blades and disruptor cannons…there was even a recon drone on the shoulder.

The cameraman had been to enough comic conventions to know faux armor when he saw it, and this was not fake. Peering closely, he could see that it even had signs of battle damage. The left shoulder had a bullet hole sewn shut. Someone had done a crude job of it, not professional at all. Then it occurred to him that his mother had a scar in that same spot. He had seen it on summer days when she would wear a tank top.

But it was the size of the suit that told him how long it had been since his mother had worn it. Although the body suits had great elasticity to them, there were limits to the laws of physics. He could not remember a time in his life when Mom would have fit into that thing.

"So much for her claims of being big-boned." He had just uttered the comment when he realized she was standing in the bedroom door. Still holding packages from the mall, she could easily see the mess he had left from his searching.

"This was really yours?" He gestured to the placard that read "RAVEN." Although he was a huge fan boy, that name did not ring a bell. But then again, this was his mother's era. *Only archeologists studied that era of superheroism.*

"So is this how Mister Marvelous knows you?" Dave understood the connection now. *Sure, they were likely on the school board together too, of course.* Supers always liked to hide in plain site as pillars of their community. That was the oldest story in the comic book.

"It's time you know who your real father is," she said with a frown.

"So Dad wasn't really killed in a factory accident?" Dave suddenly felt as if his whole world was a lie.

"No. He was married, that's why we never…" She trailed off.

"Who is he?" Dave was immediately curious.

"Here. Meet him for yourself. I'll jingle him and let him know you're going to be calling. You're old enough." Transferring him a digital scrap of paper, she gave him the contact info.

"I'm twenty-five, Mom. I was old enough years ago!" Irritated, he wanted to ask more, but the child in him insisted on stomping out of the room in a huff. Leaving the apartment, he was driving away in his rental before he could bring himself to stop. It just irritated him, the idea that she waited until he was almost 30 to tell him any of this.

He had a name and a number. The logical thing to do would have been to call the number. But being a journalist, he did what an investigative reporter does: he investigated.

A series of quick searches revealed that Clark Wayne was a children's therapist in Covina, and his home address was just a few blocks away. It was a nice neighborhood, way out of Dave's price range though. Adjusting course, Dave found himself standing on the porch minutes later. Ringing the bell, he waited patiently.

The woman that answered had a regal posture about her, as if she were an archangel sent down to live among the mortals. Her outfit was sublime, her smile warm and hospitable, yet formal.

"Where's the package?" she asked, still smiling.

"Package?" He reflected the word.

"The new bot, the Opaque 500 floor bot. Aren't you from Amazon?" She looked at him, then his tiny rental car. *Then she looked at him again.*

"Aren't you...?" She raised a Vulcan eyebrow.

"Jenna Meadows' son." Dave answered. He remembered the woman from his childhood. Although they attended some of the same school district events, she had always been in another sphere from his mother.

"I always knew this day would come." Her smile was gone, replaced by irritation. "Come in."

Dave followed, taking in the house as he went. It was a lot nicer than his own home. Although they lived just a mile apart, there was a big difference in the neighborhoods. His mother's single income budget just did not buy that much home.

He also noticed the diplomas on the wall. While many were for Clark Wayne, about half were for Georgia Hoffendorn-Wayne. The Hoffendorns were known for their money and influence in this town. They owned car dealerships, factories, and most of the city council.

Seated on the couch, Georgia Hoffendorn-Wayne had a tea-bot serving them almost as soon as they hit the cushions. Her mechanized staff was efficient and orderly, as was everything in the house. To that end, the entire home was decorated quite tastefully. Dave knew all the hallmarks of a queen bee nest; he had grown up in one himself. *No man decorated this home*, of that he was reasonably sure.

Looking over the plethora of family photos everywhere, he felt as if someone were overcompensating somehow. The images were plentiful enough that it seemed like they were trying hard to sell the myth of a happy home. He was digesting his 30th photo when he spotted a familiar face in the middle.

Although he wore glasses, there was no mistaking Mister Marvelous. While the frames fooled most people, Dave had just met the man, up close and personal, only days ago.

"He was my dad?" Dave was out of his chair, picture frame in hand.

"According to genetic tests; yes. My family paid your mother's monthly ransom...*I mean child support.*" She pretended to be polite.

"Child support?" he said absentmindedly.

"Yes, the check from Hanson Manufacturing? Every month? You are wondering why they stopped?" She was sure that was why he was here.

"Hanson   Manufacturing…?"   Dave muttered the words. "That's the company my Dad was supposed to have died at, so they sent a check every month…" He could see now that he had been lied to.

"Yes, the agreement was we pay her, and you two stay far and away. Now those rules seem to be moot." Raising her eyebrows, she implied that he was in breach of contract.

"Look, I don't know anything about that. I just came home, found out my Mom was a Super, and my Dad is Mister Marvelous, and I'm trying to keep it together. I didn't mean to bust in on you, and I'm sorry about your daughter and all. I didn't know her, except that one time she kicked me in the junk for no reason, but it was sad her getting snuffed by some random energy blast. I'm sorry, I didn't mean to intrude." Turning, Dave was halfway to the door before she jumped into his path. Surprisingly nimble for a woman of her vintage, she had raised one eyebrow in curiosity.

"You mean you *just-just* found out?" she asked, waiting for him to nod the affirmative. "But you're how old…?"

"Yeah. I know." He made a face. *Yes, he was aware that he was the buffoon who believed a lie till he was almost 30.* No need to torment the wound.

"Look, I'm being rude, please, finish your tea and tell me about yourself. You would be nearly Eustice's age, had she..." Georgia trailed off.

Dave allowed himself to be steered to a nearby chair. A bot replaced his tea with another sweetened to exactly the previous setting.

"I understand that you must feel shut-out by this whole process, but there was much at stake in this. It would have been..." She was searching for the right words when he cut her off.

"Scandal. Is that the word?" It surprised him to say the words with such force. But the last few hours had been unnerving.

"Scandal, yes, but much more." She tried to sum it up. "You do understand that he is a super hero, and that he represents this entire planet in combat against Ming the Merciless. Every man, woman, and child on this planet looks to him as their champion. This you understand as well, yes?"

"So again, it's scandal you were avoiding." It seemed pretty simple to him.

"No." Taking a deep breath, she tried to find her center before continuing. "There are other factors…"

Finally she made a frown and turned to the coffee table beside her. Pressing a hidden button, an aqua-blue force-field sprang up around them. The cameraman had read enough *League of Carnage* comic books to know the *ball of silence* when he saw it. Right away he knew that she wanted to say something that no one else must hear. Also, he was surprised that a housewife like her, even a rich one, would have access to such high-grade tech.

"Listen to me very carefully because I am only going to tell you this one time. In the beginning for each of us, we were given a specific set of instructions by our creator. Among those was a caution against mating with others like us."

The last part of what she said keyed something in his mind. As he looked at her, there was something so familiar about her voice as she lectured. He was sure he had heard it before. *So soothing yet authoritative…*

Holding up a hand, he blocked the top of her face from his view so he was only seeing her from the nose down. A split second later and he recognized that statuesque profile.

"You were…StarFire!" He sputtered, shocked to be sitting just a few feet away from the former commander of the *League of Carnage*. The interplanetary alliance of supers had stood as a force for good against all forms of evil for half a century. He had seen this woman kill dozens of bad guys in news footage…literally killed them. He had seen her break them, burn them, cut them, and once she even vaporized a guy. *Oh, yes,* he never missed the news when the *League of Carnage* was on.

"Yes." She remained calm before brushing that aside. "But our creator said that we were bound to certain rules, and if we break them, very bad things could happen to us. We did not choose this life, it was chosen for us."

This seemed incongruous to everything that the cameraman knew about Supers. By conventional wisdom, they just developed their powers naturally and used them either for good or evil. But now StarFire hinted at something much different.

"You know where your powers came from?" He showed evident surprise.

"We ALL know. There was no mystery to it, he kidnapped us and he held us in his lab for days of excruciating pain while he turned us into...super-beings. The entire time we were enduring the worst pain you can possibly imagine, he would lecture us on the rules, the boundaries, the limits. But above all, we had the *Three Rules of the Maker*. Break those, and we would spend eternity in far, far more pain than the transformation. At minimum we could have our powers stripped, which was just as bad for some." She had a far off look in her eyes as she spoke. No doubt she was thinking of friends who had tested those boundaries.

"Just ask Captain Courageous." Dave smirked at the thought.

"I dated him, before I married your father. Very handsome man, with a masterful body. But so egocentric. I think his vanity is why Professor Zero ended him in such a way; to send a clear message to the rest of us."

"Yeah, he splat-down right in the middle of Times Square on New Year's Eve, right as the ball was dropping. The whole damned galaxy was watching." Dave could see now that the message would have been effective indeed. Even Captain Courageous, plunging to his death, had sufficient time to understand the consequences of his actions.

"The first rule is that you must be true to your faction. The good must be true to the good faction, and evil must support evil domination of the galaxy. Turn from your faction and risk expulsion." She let that soak in without explaining how it was germane to their conversation.

"Secondly, we were cautioned against interbreeding because the results could be unpredictable. The product of two Supers would be an arch, and the product of two arch-nemesis would be a Super. But the product of a mixed-faction union could be good, bad, neutral, or even a squib." Holding her tea at a perfect ninety degree angle, she had delivered that information as if she were narrating one of her educational shows.

"Ooooh, again, I'm sorry for your loss. I never lost anyone, except a hamster, because he was in my pocket and I went in the bouncy castle, and…" He trailed off at that memory. It had been haunting him ever since it happened last year.

Something snapped in his mind. Looking up he raised a finger as he thought aloud.

"Soooo…If my Dad is a Super, and my Mom is a Super, then I should be an arch?" The idea fascinated him as much as it terrified him. *He liked the cool black suits, but the mission-plan sucked balls.*

"Do you have any secret evil powers?" She raised her eyebrows before continuing. "No, because you are a squib."

Trying to lay it out in his mind, he came to the next logical conclusion. "Oh, shit! Mister Marvelous was really an arch the whole time? And you had to keep it quiet so that he didn't get dropped like good ol' Courage?"

"Nooo!" Her pleasant demeanor completely disappeared as she scowled emphatically. "You are the product of the unholy union between a good and righteous man, and a filthy little henchwoman. Not even a proper arch-villainess, she was still working her way through the henchman program." There was a cackle as she found amusement in that. "But she certainly commanded dominion over the man. First she sullied him in sexual congress, then she insisted it was his baby, and did not have the decency to nip it in the bud, so to say. As if that were not enough, she even moved just a mile away, although I suspect my husband may have had a hand in that. I finally had to take legal action."

Dave remembered when that happened. He could still remember his mother shouting about the company his father had allegedly worked for, how they were cheating her, how they were treating her so badly. After that she had receded into a box of Mallomars, only to reemerge in her current expanding state. She had quit her job, and started working from home. In hindsight he could see that her spirit had been broken a little by the event. Discovering that the woman seated across from him was responsible, he suddenly felt a deep dislike for the lady.

But this time, instead of having his tantrum and stomping out before asking the hard questions, Dave sat tight. *He would stomp out when he was ready this time.*

"So some professor in a lab created us?" He tried to get clarification on that. It seemed so much less glamorous than natural evolution.

"Were you kidnapped and had your blood replaced with Chemical-X in an agonizing ordeal that spanned three days?" Contrite, she gave a rigid smile before cutting in again. "No, of course not. That's because you were not created by Professor Zero. You're a squib. You are nothing."

There was another question he wanted to ask, but the volcano inside him took over. Standing up, he started to call her a bitch when she waved a hand and used her psychic powers to slap him across the face. He had forgotten about those abilities. With psychics, you did not actually need to utter the words to insult them.

Stepping back with a hand on his face, Dave recalibrated himself as he noticed her standing up.

"So, what's the third rule?" He asked trying to change the subject as she grabbed him by the collar and hoisted him off the ground.

"Oh, that's the biggest rule of all; we are absolutely, positively, forbidden from speaking of these orders or the experiences from whence they come, even to other Supers and Arches, under penalty of death or dismemberment from powers." Squeezing steadily, she was tightening her grip around his throat.

"Your secret is safe with me." He offered in a gasp. Her grip was so powerful; like a piece of farm machinery had hold of him. Tighter and tighter she constricted him until it was obvious what she was doing.

"I have no desire to take that chance. I'm sorry; you seemed like such a nice young squib." Showing a sympathetic smile, she continued choking the life out of him.

In his own mind, Dave was terrified. He knew he was about to die, and there was no force on the planet that could stop her. She was StarFire, the mightiest of the heroines. He had once seen her rip the turret off a tank, and use it to beat down a giant robot, so his death was simply a given at this point. *Oh, it hurt so much.* He struggled hard against her grip until he was finally out of energy. Just hanging there he felt as if it was inevitable. Any second now he would be dead...*any second now*.

There was a snapping sensation as something suddenly felt so right. Sure that she had done her job, the housewife dropped him like a rag doll.

On the ground, Dave rolled over before rubbing his neck. Twisting his head around in every direction he made a funny smile.

"Oh, that's fucking great." His voice held true wonder. "I've had a krink in my neck for two weeks now from sleeping in that crooked-ass bed in D-block. Oh *mein Gott in himmel*, you just totally fixed that. Lookit, I can turn my head to the right now."

"I thought you didn't have any powers?" she asked uncertainly.

"I don't." he admitted freely. A split second later her fist collided with his face hard enough to send his entire skull flying across the room. *Luckily his body was still attached.* Somewhere in there he saw a flash of crimson energy as she had tried to amplify her punch tenfold.

Even though she had sent him flying, the force field caught him before he hit the wall. It made total sense; she intended to kill him without disturbing her perfect home.

Hovering now, she had used her bio-energy to burn away her own clothes to reveal the Duranium armor-suit that lay below. Sliding into place, her visor protected her eyes from her own energy blasts. Standing there with her fists balled up, she looked like a warrior goddess to the young man. Even at her age she still cleaned up miraculously well. *Her super suit was giving him a super woody.*

"That was my Proton-punch. The same punch I used to kill Culus Capitis with a single blow." She seemed bewildered that the cameraman was not in fragments already.

"Actually, I saw that fight on Channel One, and you had already hit him with an ocean liner and every car in the parking lot before you hit him with your Proton-punch." Clicking his jaw from side to side, Dave was trying to understand how he was still alive.

"But you're a squib...?" She was just as confused as he was.

"Wait...that was your real punch?" His brain had finished resetting as he straightened up.

"No," she said in a somber tone. Looking down, she seemed to be exhaling all of her breath. As she did, her energy levels made her glow. Finally completing a big breath, she aimed her breastplate at him and released a massive energy beam from the gem that was mounted on her chest.

"OWWWWW!" He shouted with a strong hint of irritation. The beam burned like the sun, but did no damage other than disintegrating his shirt. Although he could feel her pounding him with terawatts of energy, it wasn't his first time. Not so many days ago Wanda had used a similar weapon on him. The spectrum was almost the same. He could tell because they both rattled his teeth in the same pitch, or very close anyhow.

"Please stop that!" He didn't know why he did it, but he reached out and slapped her. *Sure, it was like slapping a stone gargoyle*, but he managed to convey his displeasure at being zapped. Immediately she stopped; surprised that such a low being had been able to stand up to what she had just dished out. By now, the Rumba should have been sweeping up his ashes.

Standing there shaking her head, her mask slowly retracted until she was looking directly at him. It surprised him to see tears coming from both eyes. The look on her face said that she had been cheated somehow, that the universe had treated her unfairly on a scale she could barely verbalize.

"My daughter, who was so bright, and so pretty, and so talented, the cosmos took her from me. But that malignant little bitch's bastard-child has the power of invulnerability. How is that fair? How is that right?"

Dave thought she needed a hug, but before he could even advance, she used her psychic powers to shove him back towards the door. Immediately the force field was gone.

"Just go, and never return. Please, I beg you. Your face is just a reminder that she's never coming back." The tears still streaming, it seemed strange to see such a powerful being as StarFire crying. She was universally accepted as being one of the bravest of the brave, a superhero's superhero. It boggled the journalist's mind to think of the forces at work within her skull. Having never lost a child, the closest he could relate was his loss of a hamster.

Silently he departed the home. While it had been criminal for her to try and kill him...*murder him really*, he could understand it to some degree. At 25, he had likely been a thorn in her side for a quarter of a century. Possibly more; *did she know about the affair before Mom got pregnant? Did other Supers find out first?* He wanted to know so many things.

But it did explain why their daughter Eustice had always hated him. No doubt mother had told her to steer clear of him for some fictional reason. The closest she ever got to him was kicking him in the balls at an inter-school social event, way back in the sixth grade. He never asked her to dance again after that.

As the rental car drove him a short ways, he looked over pictures he had snapped of the framed originals at Marv's house. Of particular interest was the fateful picture of the five girls who were killed by the blast. It had been circulated widely by the press following the event. Everyone had seen that photo, with Eustice Wayne holding the camera as she snapped the group selfie. But there was something about the image he had always thought odd. In the image, Eustice was smiling broadly, but the other four girls, all much prettier than Eustice, were jeering and making sour faces. He had long wondered what the scene had been all about. Was it the end of a long sleepover, or maybe a girls' adventure? The news said they were having a private meeting for the debate club when they died, so maybe that had been cover for their girl's time out?

He was still pondering the selfie when his rental car halted in front of the memorial. Stepping out, he let the vehicle whisk away to find parking on its own. Walking forward he stopped in front of the stone plaque built there. Beside it a woman stood with her eyes closed as if praying intently.

Something occurred to Dave as he watched her place fresh flowers at the site. Fingering his press credentials, he waited until she was clearly heading back to her car before approaching her.

"Ma'am, I'm a reporter with the Galactic Press, could I trouble you for a few questions? We're doing some research on the event, for the anniversary, and I would sure appreciate some background info; nothing too intrusive." Dave kept his voice soft. He could tell that she was likely a direct family member of one of the victims; otherwise she would not still be laying out fresh flowers every week.

The woman looked like a deer in the headlights as she examined him. No doubt the family had been hounded *ad nauseum* by the press for the last 15 years. Undoubtedly it had made her leery of journalists.

"What kind of questions?" Although she slowed in her progress, the woman kept moving towards the waiting car.

"I just wondered if the families ever get together to remember the girls. I mean, they were all five so close, like besties since the beginning. All of you parents had to be close too, right?" He tried to use the same soothing tone he had heard Polly use during interviews, but something went wrong.

"Besties?" The woman finally stopped walking. Her eyes wide, she pointed a stern finger at him. "No, no, no. Anna, Wanda, Pollyanna, and Corina were all friends, but they didn't like that little Wayne girl. She was mean to them, did bad things to them."

"But the picture…?" Dave flashed her the image.

"She staged it. They hated her. They were all smart, and popular, and they were going to go to the best colleges. But that girl, Eustice, there was something wrong with that girl." Her mouth had curved into a full frown. There was no subtlety about her on this issue.

"But the picture?" He didn't know what else to counter with. A split second later she digitally transferred him several pictures.

Scanning each, they were photos of Eustice sitting by herself far in the distance behind the girls. There were so many pictures where the trend repeated. Selfies all around the school would show the odd little girl off by herself, just a few meters distant from the girls, as if she were the world's most obvious stalker. He was just about to take a second look at the images when they faded away before his eyes. She had set the privacy filter to single-viewing, so once he had passed over them, they were deleted. What she had shown him was not intended for publication.

Looking up from his mind's eye he saw the woman driving away. While it did not explain everything, it did answer one question; the girls had not really been friends. Though he originally mistook the woman as unhinged, a picture was worth a thousand words, and she had shown him more than a dozen.

But the locals may have thought differently about the event if they had known that little Eustice was the offspring of two Supers. *No, strike that;* she was the product of two of the greatest Supers extant. In the hero world, Marvelous and StarFire would have been prom king and queen. Together they had once beat back the entire 9th fleet with nothing more than their energy suits and sheer intestinal fortitude. So it would follow that the product of such a coupling would be something special. Good or bad, you could expect their child to be absolutely spectacular. As it turned out, the blast she created when she self-immolated could be seen from orbit. *That was pretty spectacular*, he thought to himself as he remembered seeing the footage playing over and over again on the viewer when he was a kid.

Alone in front of the memorial, he used a scanner to take a sample of the ambient energy that still lingered in the blast zone. Glancing at the readings, he made a strange face. Spectrally it was unlike anything used by any of the foes Captain Marvel had faced. He was just about to run a type-match when he realized someone was standing there.

"Marv!" He started to call the man before he noticed the horned-rimmed glasses the Super now wore. Gone was his super suit, replaced by a sweater and khaki pants. Clearly Mister Marvelous was trying to be incognito. Glancing around, Dave could see they were alone.

"Yeah, don't use that name when I'm in my secret identity. It's a thin enough disguise as it is." Gesturing to the glasses he wore, Clark Wayne looked like an ordinary suburbanite grandpa. He was even wearing slippers.

"This really works?" Incredulous, Dave wondered how his cover was not blown the first time he went to work.

"If you didn't know my secret, hadn't just met me at as Marvelous the other day, you'd just think it was a crazy coincidence that I look a lot like the guy. It's the first thing people always say; *'oh, that's him,'* but then their logical mind kicks in and says *'no, it can't be, what're the odds?'* And they just keep on going thinking they saw someone who looks just like the real guy. If people really push it, I tell them I did some impersonator work to get through college. They usually leave it at that, except for the guy who paid me a million credits to come and pretend to be myself at his kid's party. Their house was in Belize, and the trips were all expense-paid, so I had no complaints about flying first class for a week in those waters, right? I used to do it every year until the kid grew up and wanted super **models** at his parties, not super **heroes**. But y'know, come to think of it, you were conceived on one of those trips to Belize. Second year I think. Your Mom and I even put on some mock battles for the audience, then later we battled for control of the water bed, if you know what I mean…"

"Yeah, I get the idea. I've seen animated porn before." Shaking off the image, he simply could not picture his mother with Marvelous. But then he thought back to that tiny little suit; *she had not always been his Mom.*

"C'mon kid. Let's get a beer." No sooner had he said the words than he had Dave by the shoulders. In an instant, they were moving faster than the human eye could even see. It was one of his super powers; quantum speed. Once in movement, they were travelling so fast that the world around them looked as if it were standing still.

Turning his head lazily, Dave felt as if he were in a dream. The buildings were rushing by incomprehensibly fast, yet if he focused he could still make out every detail and nuance. It was so fascinating that he felt giddy from the ride.

Then it suddenly ended. As if he had run into a brick wall, they stopped with a bang. The giddy sensation was replaced by nausea as he stumbled a few paces and threw up on a doormat. Wiping his mouth, he saw the banner on the door proclaiming it to be the *Proud Home of the Wayne Family*. Quickly, he realized he had just vomited on Mister Marvelous' front doormat.

"Awwww geez! Not there!" Yanking his son by the shirt, Marv pulled Dave away from the front door. "She was pretty mad before, I can only imagine what she'll do when she finds puke all over the new door mat. Are you sure you are totally, totally invulnerable? And I mean totally? If she fires up those eye-lasers of hers, she could go Ginsu-chef on your ass, slice you up like a plate of sushi."

"So you already know that I was there today?" Dave asked as he followed Marv through the shrubberies.

"Yeah I know!" He roared over his shoulder. Why the hell do you think I'm wearing slippers? I got home, put my comfy shoes on, and the sun went supernova. I barely got out of there alive." His expression was dour before he pressed one of the landscaping rocks. Immediately the floor dropped out from under them as they seemed to fall for the longest time. Then with a thud, Dave hit the ground on his shoulder. Beside him, Mister Marvelous had made a classic hero landing.

"I had to add a DNA scanner to that switch after my gardener Manuel fell down in here and broke his leg. Their motto is *'no stone unturned'* but I thought it was just a metaphor. Apparently it's more than just a slogan. He got better though."

"Where are we?" Dave asked the question at roughly the same time his brain realized the answer. He could see the row of power suits in stasis cases, and a massive mainframe computer that scanned the galaxy for crime. It was clear, even to the casual observer that they were in the inner sanctum. "Is this…is this your lair?"

"Welcome to Paradise City, the place where the grass is green and the girls are pretty." Holding out his hands, the aging grandfather seemed like a poor spokesman for such vices.

"Girls?" Dave asked, not surprised that the man was an adulterer. After all, his own conception had been the result of the hero's philandering.

"Sure do, I got the most beautiful girls in the whole dang multiverse, don't I, darling?" Looking up, he waited with a smile.

Finally one of the holographic screens flickered to light, rendering an attractive face with piercing red eyes.

"Hello Dave." She purred in a tone reminiscent of HAL.

"Yeah, hi." The cameraman gave a distracted wave to the computer before darting towards the stasis cases. Through the transparent doors he could see the legendary equipment that had literally not aged a day since it was last used. The stasis chambers saw to that.

"Ooooh, that's the centennial armor you wore against Malignant."

"No, that's the backup suit. Tommy Hilfinger made me two of those, just in case. Malignant completely ruined the other suit with a metallic virus. The whole suit just dissolved the day after the battle. I was still making payments on the damned thing."

"Where's your wife's suits?" Dave wondered aloud.

"Her lair here with me? *No, nein, nyet-nyet.* Only one Super per lair. The only time you can have more than one hero, or heroine's gear in one lair is if they are part of something like *League of Carnage.* The other reason is for a sidekick, support staff, or a henchman. So if her lair was here, and my lair was here, then that would make one of us the sidekick, and based on sales revenue, she'd win. She totally has the female 18-40 demographic locked down tight, and she does very well in the same category for males, so that means that I'd be the bitch in that jail cell."

"Oh." It seemed a terribly shallow consideration to Dave. The more he saw of the man, the more it seemed that vanity was a central component to Clark Wayne's personality.

"Do you ever throw out old suits…?" Dave kidded. "Don't call the Salvation Army or anything, they're too busy. Just gimme a ring, I'll come take those dirty old *thangs* off your hand."

The two men shared a laugh as they appreciated the joke. The suits in the cases were more than fabric garments. Their exo-armor was beyond military grade, and the life support systems could practically keep you alive at the heart of a nuclear explosion. The least of them would have fetched billions, so it was funny to compare them to some curbside donations.

"Say, would you like to try one?" Handing his son a cold beer, Marv had his fake glasses off as he gestured to the #3 case.

"The Bunker Hill 300??" Dave felt as if the air had been sucked out of his diaphragm. There, of all the suits was the Sistine Chapel of armor suits. Marvelous had worn it when he teamed up with the *League of Carnage* and *Heroes from Hell* to fight the Magna Turci. The massive leviathan was so immense that his suit was essentially a flying battleship.

"You could destroy a planet with a suit like that." Marv poked at the glass door where it hung.

"Could I really?" Dave was suddenly concerned that he could accidentally press the wrong button.

"Well, not without the proto-plasma cannon, but if she were fully equipped, sure. I shoved Ceres into Earth orbit using that cannon. It's a theme park now." He agreed reaching to open the glass case.

But Dave was there first and yanked on the handle. Without a hiccup the coded door opened up for the cameraman.

"It sees the genealogical match." Dave observed.

"Yeah, back when I first built this place I wanted to be able to share all this with my children some day, so I must have set the encoders for me and my children, if I ever had any." Marv was about to reach in to pull the suit down off the rack when he felt the rush of air as someone moved behind him. Instinctively he moved to shield Dave before using his quantum speed to shove the cameraman out of the way.

But he never got the chance. Wanda's crimson energy beam hit Dave broadsides, sending him flying into a wall. He never even knew he was under attack. One moment he was reaching out for the Bunker Hill 300, and the next his world was filled with birdies and stars. After that there was some blackness as his brain tried to reboot.

Marvelous had started to advance on the woman in black, but she used one blast to pitch him into the air, followed by another that sent the elderly hero flying. After passing through a security door, a maintenance door, a guardrail, and a flight of stairs, he finally came to rest at the bottom of the stairwell.

"Waiter, could I get an espresso at this table, please." He held up a single finger before collapsing back into the heap of debris.

For his own part, Dave was leaning into a gigawatt worth of energy pouring out of each of Wanda's fists. Clearly she was trying to incinerate him, but it was not working at all. Still, the pain was incredible. Although his newfound power kept him from dying, it still hurt like hell when she blasted him. He felt every bit of it.

Seeing that her energy beam was having no effect, she used her purple energy stream to capture and hold him while she thrashed him bodily against the concrete floor. Shouting in rage as she slammed him against the cement, her words seemed almost incoherent...at least what Dave could hear of it as his head was repeatedly banged against the floor. Hearing only snippets between the impacts, all he could make out was ***POW*** *you bastard* ***BAM*** *get your own Father!* ***KERPOW*** *who do you think you are?* ***CRUNCH BANG SMASH***.

But even as he was being Hulk-thrashed, he could not help but notice that the energy she used against him had a familiar spectral hue to it.

Dave felt strange in that moment. He was being blasted with the power of a small sun, or at least it felt that way, and all the while being flailed against the ground and ceiling alternately. Yet the whole time he had become inured to the whole experience. Sure, once he had been terrified. But now it was a little boring. The only upside to it was that he had an idea how to leverage his seemingly useless powers. Already he could feel her grip loosening on him. It took a significant amount of power to do what she was doing, and power is not infinite. Slowly, bit by bit, she was weakening until finally she dropped him to the ground. Panting, she kept firing individual pulses as fast as she could recharge herself. Really it was the portrait of futility; if her concentrated hand beams could not harm him, then the pulses were unlikely to do more than mess his hair.

Striding across the floor between blasts, Dave was finally close enough to reach out and slap the woman. Though he had no super powers, he really leaned into that smack. It must have been a good slap because she stopped shooting and held a hand to her cheek in surprise.

Dave was just about to point out how they should communicate like adults when she jammed her fist forward. He could see her charging her capacitors for a massive blast, so he did the only thing he could think of; he punched her.

No, not another slap, and not a normal Dave punch. Nope, this time he imagined Captain Legend delivering one of his patented Krypton punches and emulated that. Grabbing her by the side of her head, he had delivered a stunning, center-mass punch to her face. The result was that he knocked the arch-villainess to the ground in a big leather pile.

At first he thought he had activated one of her countermeasures or something; her head looked totally different…like it was glowing in a golden hue? Confused, he held up his fist and realized that he was gripping a full head of black hair. Attached to it was Wanda's jet-black mask.

"This is…" He mumbled, realizing he was holding wig. Only then did it occur to him that he had pulled off her disguise.

Looking down at her, he found himself looking at Wanda without her mask. What he saw made him gasp in surprise.

"You're fired!" She spat out the words before rubbing her nose where he had punched her.

"Polly?" Dave stood upright in shock. Although he had noticed the physical resemblance before, the idea that one could actually be the other was preposterous. *Simply impossible.* One was made from sugar & spice, the other was made from pure, distilled evil. Yet here he was face to face with that truth.

As he tried to wrap his head around this newfound knowledge, something occurred to the cameraman. Using the little scanner from his pocket, he saw that her energy was a match for the sample he had taken from the memorial site. *It had been her power that had killed those girls.*

"You're Eustice Wayne!" He pointed out the revelation. "You didn't die that day; you incinerated those girls!"

Her expression showed distaste before she slowly morphed into a young schoolgirl in a blue uniform. Pretty, and with a great smile, she had been one of the girls in the selfie.

"Oh, we're all in here still." Giving a curtsy, her smile faded to hatred. "We all get to come out and play, when she needs us."

Another morph and she was back to Polly. It took a second of looking at her face anew to realize it was simply one of the schoolgirls, all grown up. Wanda was the fourth girl, plus twelve years. The answer had been right in front of them all these years. Small wonder she was a hit on the regional TV stations: she had the face of a local fallen angel.

"It's not what you think." There was an iron hand on his shoulder. Looking up he saw Marv standing there.

"She killed four people? How can you put a slant on that?" Dave knew it was harsh, but true.

"I had no control over my powers, and no one told me to expect super powers so when they happened I thought I was...defective, and I tried to keep it in, but that day they were harassing me and it was just too much." Shaking, Polly looked like she was fighting the urge to empty her capacitors on the cameraman.

"They were bothering **you**?" Dave asked, having heard a much different story.

"They used to stalk me, at lunch, passing periods. If I was in the library reading, they would take a table nearby and take selfies and say things and taunt me. The bitches even joined the debate team just so they could harass me. Well, they just picked the wrong day, and I blew. I had no control over my power, didn't even know I was supposed to be trying to control it."

"Why the hell not?" Dave looked to his newfound father. "For that matter why didn't you tell me? I mean, with her there was a fifty-fifty chance she was gonna blow…up…" His words tapered off as he suddenly understood Marv's logic for keeping it secret.

"Yeah, how do you tell a kid that they are either going to turn into one of the Arches in her comic books, or just detonate like a thermonuclear bomb one day. No pressure, right?" Marv used colloquial terms, but the point was accurate. "Not only that, but she was illegal. The Leagues had all banned Supers from having babies because they were worried it could tilt the balance in the wrong direction, so when Star had our baby, we told people she was adopted, said she was the last survivor of a family who was wiped out by evil. There had actually been a baby found at the battle of Costco, but I dropped that kid off at an orphanage on the way home. Told everyone that was her, and we hoped for the best." Helping Polly up, Marvelous tried to convey his concerns for the young lady. Like any father, he was her truest advocate.

"Yeah, and I've been the one who was here, who was loyal to…" She thought better of her words before activating a Ball of Silence around them. "I have been the daughter who has been here every day, supporting the cause and being the double-agent, but do you let me wear the Bunker Hill? NO! You said it was special armor, not even **you** wear it anymore, but you were about to let squib-boy there put it on!"

"You were a double agent all along?" There was awe in the cameraman's voice. "So that's why you didn't kill me when you blasted me back at Ming's. I see now."

Without warning, Polly delivered a solid right cross, snapping his head around.

"No, I meant to kill you back there. You were the reason my parents almost got divorced, and the cause of him sleeping down here so many nights. Removing you from the world would have made it the galaxy a better place."

"I get that a lot." Dave remembered StarFire trying to snap his neck earlier that day.

"Can we kiss and make up?" Marvelous offered cheekily. He was concerned about any further damage to his lair. Toys were expensive, and it was hard to sneak the money from his wife.

Something bothered Dave about the whole scheme.

"If you have her...fucking Ming, then why hasn't she just cut his throat and won the war? Hasn't that been the whole purpose of the Supers, to one day depose him and install a galactic democracy?" Dave squinted at the two of them. Although he read a lot of comic books, he was pretty sure that philosophical tidbit had come from the newspapers. But it could have been written by Stan Lee for all he knew.

"First off, I never fucked that miserable old man. I'm not even sure he has a functioning penis." Polly wanted to clear the air on that. "Secondly, we have a much bigger mission. Ming is just part of the construct. Like us, his strings are being pulled by Professor Zero. There's a much bigger mission at hand." Polly dismissed her step-brother as a *noob*.

"Professor Zero?" Dave stuttered at the name. "That's a real thing? Who's HIS boss? Some psychic professor in a wheelchair?"

"Don't mock what you don't know." Squinting hatefully at her brother, Polly was still unhappy to have the cameraman here. Up until now, this had been a place where she had exclusive access to her Daddy. But now there was an interloper in the scene, and it galled her to no end. Her adult mind knew it was not really any of Dave's fault; but there was no erasing the feelings she had grown up with. Mister Marvelous was **her** father, and she had no desire to share!

As if Dave needed any reminding of the marital problems his birth had caused, he could see a messy cot in the far corner. It looked like the thing had seen some serious use over the years.

"So are you going to tell me about this real mission of yours, or do I have to wait another twenty-five years to learn the truth about that too?" Folding his arms, Dave gave his father a grimace. He knew there was no point appealing to Polly while she was in this mood.

"Cop a squat." Gesturing to a stool at the bar, Marvelous slid into the bartender's slot. "Look-see, the Supers and Arches have been showing up on the landscape for about fifty years now. They started small, some never made it past the local papers, others grabbed world headlines, and a few like me eventually grew to galactic fame. But we're no accident of evolution."

"I know about the professor who kidnapped you and gave you the three rules and all that jazz-hands bullshit. I'm not one of you artificial mutants so the three rules mean nothing to me." Dave sipped his beer as he sat at the end of the bar.

Marv considered this before continuing with his story. "At first we all pretended as if the lie was true, that we were natural evolution, but then over the years we broke the third rule and started talking amongst ourselves about how we came to be Supers and Arches. Yes, it was the same for the Arch-villains too."

"So we have some professor guy running around the galaxy creating new heroes and villains, what…twenty times a year or more?" Dave tried to put it into practical terms.

"More like a hundred times." Marv looked down sadly. "Not everyone survives the process. You only hear about the successes, but the obituaries are full of the failures. This guy, this Professor Zero, he is essentially running the galaxy like a puppet regime."

"But Ming runs the place…?" Dave was still trying to wrap his head around the idea.

"I told you; Ming is just part of the construct. He's like us, but built specifically to rule, and subject to the same three rules." Scowling, Polly sat at the other end of the bar.

There was a long silence as Clark Wayne, sans glasses, slowly slid an umbrella-topped blue drink down to his daughter. Holding his beer, Dave gave her girly drink a smug look.

Polly detected her brother's subtle mockery and pretended to ignore the drink before looking surprised. "Where's my beer?"

"But honey, you hate beer." Marv frowned. "This is your fav; Blue Mandarins."

"I usually drink…Scotch, and Everclear. I only drink these when I'm here…because I need to stay sharp." Nodding as if it helped cover the fabrication, Polly pretended like she preferred the hard stuff.

"You're Wanda B. Wicked. I'd expect you drank gasoline with bits of crushed glass in it." Rolling his eyes, Dave wished his sister would get over herself.

"Flaming gasoline," she added before stuffing the black wig and mask back down over her blonde curls. She did a bad job of it, leaving blonde hair jutting out from under her wig.

"So what is this mission?" Dave tried to guess. "Go out and find this guy who is creating supers and do what, exactly? Kill him? Make him create only Supers? Make him stop creating anything at all?"

"To restore democracy to the galaxy." Marvelous stood upright as he saluted an old American flag that hung on the far wall. Somewhere in the background the soundtrack for Gettysburg could be heard playing.

There was a long moment as he stood there, looking like the all-American hero, with the music playing in the background, and the bar lights silhouetting him. But Polly and Dave simply exchanged looks as each rolled their eyes in turn. The man was a consummate showman; and clearly he did not know when to turn it off.

"So that's it?" Dave blinked twice. "Really?"

"Really, really." Wanda made a playfully mocking face.

"But why would you wanna do that? You're an Archess. Shouldn't you be trying to swing things the other way?" Skeptical of his sister's motivations, he queried further. "So what then? You find this guy, and he doesn't take away your powers or vaporize you with *waaaaay* better powers, then what? Kill him? Imprison him? That'd probably be like trying to keep universal solvent in a jar." Shaking his head, he showed his disapproval.

Watching his father and sister consider what he had just said, Dave thought it wise to point out a few more details.

"Not only that, but once you kill this guy, there will still be a few thousand Supers and Arches out there. Enough to screw things up for the next sixty years. I mean, have you considered what happens if the last man standing is an Arch? And really, what's wrong with things the way they are now? I mean, that's quite the arrangement you have set up with Ming." Turning to Polly, the cameraman revealed what he had seen on the surviving camera. "He meets with Ming and they work out the battle, the outcome, and even the legislative compromise. You can watch the video yerself."

Dave pushed the segment to her via his nannites. He could see her eyes darting around as she previewed the footage in her head.

"You're fucking my chief minion!" With fiery eyes, Wanda turned to her father. "You promised you'd stop sleeping around!"

"I...she totally came onto me, and I was weak, I admit it, but what was I to do? Your mom ignores me for a decade at a time, and your minion was all over me like a sex-cat-thing, and there was nothing I could do." Marv did his best to defend himself.

"I keep her chained in a cell in the basement of the ship when I'm not using her. How in the hell could she have been all over you? You dirty, old man." Admonishing him with her eyes, Wanda shook her head in disgust.

"Okay, I admit it, I saw her in the cell, she looked lonely, and she seemed to like it. I mean, she never said no." A warm smile crossed his face as Marv remembered the night.

"Of course she never objected; her mouth is sewn shut!" Slamming down her drink hard enough to dislodge the umbrella, Wanda made it obvious that this was not the first time the two had this fight before.

"Not…anymore." Sheepishly, Marv admitted that last detail.

"Why on Earth would you unstitch her mou…OOH you pervert!" Wanda figured it out in the middle of her own question.

"Three words: Ice cube blowjob." Marvelous had turned to enlighten his son on the practice. "She's a natural, being dead and all, she's naturally cold as a dead fish."

"Ooh my Zog." Wanda had her head in hands as if she had a sudden migraine. "That is sooo disgusting, how can you even find her attractive? She's reanimated dead."

In his own mind Dave remembered the sleek little minion who had carried the case during their last encounter. Once you got past those crazy-dead eyes of hers, and the stitched up mouth, she was pretty hot.

"I'd hit that." Dave shrugged before getting a knuckle-bump from his father.

"What doesn't kill you..." A grin in place, Marv left it for them to finish the old saying.

"...Gives you zombie herpes." Her mouth forming a grimace, Wanda was serious this time.

"That's a real thing?" Marv froze in place, his eyes wide.

"Yes, it is. Don't give it to Mom!" Clearly irritated, Wanda wanted to unload her capacitors on her father. Truly, she had liked him better when she didn't know he was really a super hero.

"Oh, no chance of that." Marv nodded. "The last time I got to see your Mom naked was when Theros burned off her suit at the battle of Marcos, and I had to watch that on TV because I was in Syuné saving some lemmings from tooth decay. Damned PSAs."

Giving him the evil eye, Polly grumbled a curse under her breath. Changing the topic, Mister Marvelous took the conversation in another direction.

"What we have reached is actually very close to democracy. Ming respects the challengers, so he makes legislative accommodations, and in the end we affect the process." Marv explained. "But we keep chasing the bubble because every time we get close to any kind of democratic rule, Professor Zero changes the balance, tilts the pinball table in his favor."

"Remember the first rule." Wanda pointed out before sipping her Blue Mandarin.

"Yeah," Marv agreed. The Professor has been known to show up and order Arches and heroes to do specific things. He assigns his own quests, and you either obey, or…"

"Captain Courageous." Dave knew the answer. He could not help but wonder what it was the Captain had refused to do.

"If this were a situation where we had achieved some type of feudal balance in our whole galactic legal system, then we would be okay with it." Marv beamed, illustrating the fact that he had a great spot in the process.

"But even Ming gets orders to do things he hates to do." Wanda sat forward, suddenly eager to share her own knowledge. "I managed to beat it out of him a few times, the things he has been forced to do. Bel-Nor, Korth, Ruban. And I've met other Arches who had been made offers they couldn't refuse."

"You remember Hugh G Member? Word is he used to be Zero's bitch, but when he tried to get out…" Marvel trailed off, knowing that his son could fill in the blanks.

"He ended up impaled on the spike atop the Dubai Towers. No one noticed him until the sun came up." Dave was in awe as he remembered that. "I always thought Quasar Man did that before he vanished off the grid."

"Nah, Quasar had been dead a year from cancer when Hugh got it." There was a solemn look on Marv's face.

"Really?" Dave felt another of his realities being shattered.

"I was pallbearer at his funeral. Nailed the widow later that night, too." Clark Wayne sucked in his gut and puffed out his chest as he positively beamed at the memory. "So many widows, so little Marvelous to go around."

Wanda gave him a vengeful look but said nothing. It was obvious that she disliked her father's philandering. Briefly she wondered if she was wrong to have hated Dave and his mother all these years when the real problem was her own father.

Waving her hands as the men chatted; Wanda was tired of the conversation.

"None of this discussion matters. We have a plan, and it's in the final planning stages, so we don't need help from civilians." Her eyes rested squarely on her brother.

"Oh, lemme guess; you're going to go in there with him as your prisoner," Dave made air quotes as he spoke that last word. "Make Ming think you captured his arch enemy, then suddenly he takes off the restraints and you capture Ming. Maybe you should take a thermal detonator with you too, Princess Leia."

Marvelous's jaw dropped open as his glasses slipped forward. Still seated at the bar, Wanda had her face in her hands as she made a moaning sound.

"Wow, you must have stumbled across my secret plans somewhere." Clark Wayne seemed serious.

"I told you it was a stupid plan." Wanda lashed out at her father. Reaching up, she yanked off her mask and wig before burying her face in the nook of her elbow. "I think I picked the wrong week to quit sniffing glue."

"That is a perfectly good plan, and it has almost worked several times." Marvelous pointed out that fact as if it were proof.

"**Everyone** tries that trick with Ming." Her voice muffled, Polly still had her face buried in her arm.

"Well, I don't see you with a better idea." Defensive, the old man raised his voice slightly.

As the father and daughter fell into another of their arguments, Dave had chosen to stroll by a wall where Marvelous had equipment stored on neat little racks and holders. It all looked so perfect, the way the proton blaster fit into its spot right between the dermal regenerator and the Blade of Angost. There were so many bits of hardware hanging on that wall. There were stunners, and zombie buttons, and kinetic grenades... The list went on and on. It was practically a *who's who* of advanced weaponry.

Turning back, he could still hear them arguing over their plan. Nowhere near a resolution, they would likely argue for hours. But as much as Dave enjoyed hanging with the Supers, there was something that had been gnawing at him for hours; Mom.

It had been a roller-coaster ride for him since he came home. First he found out his mother was a Super, then he learned the identity of his real father, then he found out his mother really wasn't a Super…she was an Arch! For hours he had been trying to relate to her situation back then. But after mulling over the 3-rules he was beginning to make sense of it all.

He doubted Marv & Wanda even noticed he had ducked out. Still debating the best way to kidnap to Ming, they had been deep in discussion, with maps and charts laid out on the bar.

Once home, he found his mother on the couch watching her shows. That had been her life for years; work for ten hours, then come home and fall asleep to the TV.

With a flick of her hand, she turned off the TV as soon as he entered the room. Dave knew that was her sign that she wanted to talk about something serious. *Most of the time she wouldn't even pause her shows.*

"I'm so sorry that I never told you all these years, but I didn't want to put pressure on you, especially when it turned out you were a…" She trailed off, not wanting to say the word.

"Squib." You didn't want to tell me about the powers, because if I didn't get them, then it would have crushed me. Ignorance was bliss, right?" Sitting down, he understood why she had kept that secret. "But what I don't understand is why you left. I mean, you were an Arch. I looked you up; You were an official bad-ass! You could fly…and you had Mega-Punch."

"Oh," She blushed before slapping her belly. "Now I'm just plain old Mega!"

She could see that her joke was not going to derail his question. Taking a moment to sum up her feelings, she finally spoke again.

"I just wanted to do other things with my life." She lied.

"I know about Professor Zero." he revealed.

His mother's expression changed immediately. Looking around nervously, she reached up and yanked the top button off her blouse. Throwing it down, the button immediately enveloped them in a Ball of Silence.

"Holy fuck, does everyone have these things but me?" Dave was aghast.

"They do if they talk about…*him*." Even in the BoS she whispered, ever cautious. "He monitors us; we never know when he's listening. He has a thousand eyes and he sees everything."

"Mom?" Dave was growing concerned. "I understand that you left the empire so you could give me a life as a normal child. I want you to know I love you for it, and appreciate it." Using phrases he had learned in a human-dynamics class, he wanted his mother to know that her sacrifice was not forgotten.

"Oh…" She made a funny smile before waving a hand. "I didn't leave because of you. I left because I just wasn't cut out to be an Arch. It's just not me. Really, I wanted to be a nurse or a physical therapist, but Zero said that's helping people, which is against the values of my faction, so I couldn't do it. The best I could do was work for the government, because even though I try to help people, they just get screwed in the end anyhow. It's all I can do. If you leave the syndicate, there isn't a lot that you can do."

"You can't just walk away?" Dave was surprised at this. But then again it made sense; if the professor went through all the effort of kidnapping and mutating these subjects, then he would not want to give up that work.

"It's difficult. I'd rather have been a Super; I like helping people, but that son of a bitch Zero insisted I was an Arch…and that bitch StarFire was a hero. I went to college with her, that sorority cu…she was an asshole back then." Her ire was definitely up.

"StarFire? She tried to kill me today." Dave nodded. "Ahh, the good times."

"Kill you? Is that why you smell like burnt polyester?" Sitting back, she fumed. "He took us both at the same time. Kept us in the lab, one across from the other. For three days of pure torture I had to look at that uppity whore. He kept telling us that we could die from the procedure, and there were bodies stacked in the freezer, I saw 'em. The whole time though, the only thing that kept me going was wanting to outlive that sorority slut. No way in hell was I gonna die before she did. When it was all over, we got dumped on a street corner with a super suit and the three rules. The first thing she did when we got free was to kick me and run away. I wish I'd thought of that first."

"He took you together?" Dave's face screwed up in thought as he tried to understand why someone would do that. While it may seem efficient to process two at the same time, it also risked exposure. It meant kidnapping two girls, which was twice as likely to be found out or interrupted.

"He took lots of people together. Sometimes he even took entire groups of people together and converted them. He'd drop the dead bodies in one place, and the living ones in another. Hugh G. said there were thirty strangers in his group. Some Supers, some Arches. It was like he was on a deadline or something."

"So all these years you've been in this miserable job because he won't let you do what you want to do?" Trying to focus on the important parts, the young photojournalist understood why the woman had given up on herself. Focused on raising her child, she had little else to fill her soul. Her work was a meaningless shuffle of paperwork, and every time a new administration took over she had to start all over again. Like Sisyphus, she spent her days rolling a useless boulder up a hill. Her only respite was her son and her TV shows.

"We're…we're gonna change that." Nodding, Dave seemed to be thinking of something a million miles away. "I gotta go back to work."

She started to question him, but only got a kiss on the top of her graying head before he was out the door.

The Plan of the Century

By the time Dave got back to Marv's lair, the ball of silence had grown almost to the same size as the lair. This was to accommodate the additional heroes who had arrived in his absence. Glancing around, he counted almost twenty of the armor-clad Supers all camped out in chairs or leaning against walls. There in the middle of the room was a holographic map of the *Mors Machina*. Pointing out access points as she lectured was StarFire. Clad from head to toe in immaculate-white armor, she was quite a sight.

Somewhere in the back of the room Mister Marvelous stood glumly in the corner while his wife stole the show. He had known it would happen as soon as it became evident that they needed her help to pull off the plan.

They had worked together enough times that he knew his wife would stomp in there, wearing her power armor, and take charge of things. Right away she would decide that his whole plan was *absolute crap*, and come up with one of her own that sounded vaguely like the original plan. It had been the story of his married life. She was the only person in the galaxy who could steal the spotlight from him. But still, as he watched his wife striding back and forth, so firmly in her element and ready for mortal combat, that he was reminded him why he had pursued her in the first place. He had to admit, even by his standards she was a goddess, worthy of worship.

Across the room, Dave stood and listened to the incredibly intricate plan being laid down by their new leader. Although he remained silent, he wanted to shout out *"He's seen this before! Episodes sixty-two, seventy-one, and the special bonus double-issues ninety-nine and one hundred. Everything you are planning is just the same old bullshit!"*

But he knew that he was the FNG, the *fricking new guy*. Most still thought he was a squib, the rest thought he was the bastard child of an Arch. *Hell, he didn't even have a suit.* No one was going to listen to him.

Instead, he stood staring at the equipment board. He had been fermenting an idea in the back of his mind ever since leaving his mother's house. Since then he had run through it a dozen times and found no appreciable problems. By his reckoning, it was best if they continued to consider him a squib. He would need every advantage possible.

Reaching out he grabbed two of the zombie buttons off the board; a red one and a blue one. Another few steps and he opened the stasis chamber in the middle. Plucking out the suit within, he knew exactly which armored outfit he wanted. Having grown up fantasizing about this very question, he had long ago answered the question of which of Mister Marvelous' battle-suits would he choose. Obviously he wanted the suit with flying powers, and something to make him *not* punch so much like a girl…and **missiles**! Yes, that had always been one of the basic criteria. He had long ago eliminated any suit that did not at least have anti-armor AP rounds.

And there was one suit that filled his wildest dreams; *Excalibur*.

It was lighter than he had expected, with the golden metal weave and Valerian steel armor. Soft as cotton, yet capable of stopping a train, it was undeniably the perfect suit. And it was thin enough that it could be worn under his street clothes.

Sure to scoop up a few boxes of ammo, he silently left without saying a word. No one noticed or objected, they were all too busy watching StarFire's briefing. In fact, *Captain Chaos* held open the door for him when he saw Dave's hands were full.

"Thanks, man." The cameraman was curt, even as he realized that he had just met one of his earliest childhood heroes. The man had been on every box of Wheaties for a year. Dave had once even tried to tattoo Chaos's face on his arm with an ink marker, but that only got him beat up at the bus stop.

Still plotting and planning in his head, Dave made it all the way to his car before he stopped and looked back towards the man who had just held open the door for him.

"You're dead…I was at your funeral…" He said to no one as he stood at the door of his shuttle. It occurred to him that they had likely faked Chaos' death for standard reasons. Either it was part of a forthcoming plot, or they needed an excuse to get all of the Supers together for a meeting. He knew from studying these people that although their plans were elaborate, they tended to think along the same lines, over and over again. *Super-duper powers, teeny-tiny imaginations*.

Stashing Excalibur in his luggage, he arrived at the *Mors Machina* and found his place in employee parking. Strolling a short ways, he had been working on some paperwork during the trip. Stopping in front of the reservation desk, he plunked down the documents for the Morganeese clerk to process.

"You gonna take the *Sexus Navis* out?" The guard seemed perplexed by the request, and for good reason: this was Ming's personal pleasure craft. The fornication that was rumored to have occurred on the decks of that ship were the stuff of legends. Ming loved that ship more than his own minions. He had once executed a servant for bleeding on the upholstery, so the staff had always viewed that ship apart from all others.

However, the Morganeese were not clerks; they were killers and leg-breakers. But once behind a desk they were relatively easy to manipulate. Dave had equated them to NPCs, or non-player characters. Yes, the Morganeese had a genius for war, but they had absolutely zero resources for much else.

"Wha's up?" A sergeant appeared, a heavy missile launcher on his back.

"Eee wants' ta take the *Sexus* out." There was a hint of uncertainty to the guard's voice. It was as if he knew there was something atypical about it all, but could not quite place his big, bulbous finger on it.

"Do 'e got the paperwork?" The noncom asked calmly.

Waving the sheets of paper, the private confirmed that fact.

"Den we make 'd reservation. It's whats they tolds me when I started; if dey gots da' paperwork, den dey can takes da' ships." Shrugging, the old sergeant explained his deepest understanding of the post orders.

"Reservation approved!" Shrugging, the clerk used a big rubber stamp to mash an approval across the top of the document.

"Have a good day, Sergeant." Dave smiled and waved as he headed back to his room in D-block.

He spent the next two days sitting around the big palace ship. Polly was still pretending to be barricaded in her apartment. As far as anyone knew, she was still in the midst of her Diva attack and would be out within the week. The staff reported that she was indeed eating her meals, and even requesting extra foodstuffs and deserts, so logically she must really be in there. The dishes were certainly piling up outside her door.

But Dave had an idea who was eating all the food while his sister was still off-ship. If he guessed right, the food was being consumed by a certain little member of the UZLD Community [undead zombie living-dead]. With the stitches removed from her mouth she had likely rediscovered eating in a big way.

And while he waited, Dave did what any good cameraman would do; he took miles and miles of footage. A show like theirs would have lots of little spots that need filler or transitions. *At least that was his excuse for hanging around with all the cameras*. Really he was just biding his time until things fell into place.

"What are you up to? Are you planning something?" Like a tin-pot dictator, Lotus had become suspicious for no apparent reason.

"Yeah, planning on paying my rent." Dave smarted back at the henchman.

"What's that supposed to mean? Did someone pay you to bring weapons onboard the ship?" Grabbing Dave's hand, Lotus examined the camera with his beady eyes.

"Your Dad pays me to take footage. I already took three days off. What am I supposed to do? Not work just because Polly is on her period?" Shrugging, Dave never flinched.

"Does Polly ever mention me?" Lotus' entire demeanor had changed on a dime. Slinking up close to the cameraman he seemed curious about the reporter. "Sometimes I get the impression that she's hot for me."

"Yeah, you don't gotta worry about that." Giving the henchman a skeptical look, Dave continued to mount a camera to one of the columns.

"Oh, did she say something?" Suddenly interested, Lotus brushed back his greasy hair.

Rolling his eyes, Dave gave a sigh. "Yeah; she said she'd rather be trapped in an elevator with Justin Bieber than date you."

"Oh, that's especially harsh." The minion stopped dead in his tracks as he felt the insult. Although he did not say a word, it was obvious that Dave had wounded him deeply.

Thinking better of it, the cameraman had an idea.

"But you know who does have the hots for you?" Dave raised his eyebrows happily. "Callie Cadaver!"

There was a moment of brief uncertainty on the henchman's face before as he tried to place the name.

"You know, Wanda's chief hench-woman." Dave gently reminded him.

"Really…" There was obvious hesitancy on Lotus' face as he thought of the little undead woman who followed Wanda about.

"Oh yeah, didn't you notice how she was totally eyeballing you last time she was here. She knows a winner when she sees one." Giving a wink, Dave put his seal on it.

"But…she's reanimated dead isn't she…?" Clearly skeptical, the minion seemed hesitant as he thought of the little dead girl with the crazy eye.

"Oh, that girl is a total freak once you get a few Jell-O shots into her." Keeping his voice low, Dave acted as if he were sharing a secret.

"Lotus likes freaks…" Speaking of himself in the third person, the chief minion was slowly embracing the idea.

"Oh yeah, no one parties like dead chicks. Everyone knows that." Dave nodded as if it were common knowledge. "Word is, you take her out somewhere nice, feed her a couple pounds of brains, and you'll need a crowbar to get her off of you."

"Really…?" Scratching his chin, Lotus seemed lost in lustful thoughts. "But what about Wanda?"

"What about her?" Dave raised an eyebrow.

"Wanda kills me practically every time she comes aboard." Exasperated, Lotus confided in the cameraman.

"Oh, she's just being protective like a mama-bear. Y'know? You just gotta win her over, is all." Patting the minion on the back, Dave left him dreaming of the little dead girl.

Subtle things began to tell Dave that the attack was still on schedule. First there was the waiter that looked exactly like Captain Ultimate wearing glasses and a tux. Then there was the lady mopping the floor who was clearly Omega Girl. She too was wearing a pair of horned-rimmed glasses as a key part of her disguise.

Everywhere he looked on the ship, he spotted people he recognized. The downside was that they weren't all Supers. He had also noticed dozens of well known arch-villains in the mix as well, all thinly disguised with horned rim glasses. It was a regular who's-who of the crime fighting community. While StarFire may have had her elaborate *master plan,* it was clear that Ming was posturing for battle as well.

It had occurred to Dave that the reason he was left to wander about was that both sides wanted the camera coverage. He knew he was safe; their vanity would never allow them to battle without at least a few selfies. Neither the Supers, nor the Arches ever killed the cameraman. They liked their publicity too much.

Dave was in the throne room checking the lighting when the big news came in. A larger-than-life hologram flashed into life in the middle of the room; it was Wanda. Standing ten feet tall, she towered dramatically over the people watching.

"My love, I have a *suuuurprise* for you." She smiled wickedly before yanking Marvelous up into the picture by his hair. "I caught this one somewhere he should not have been. I thought we could enjoy him together, perhaps tear a pheasant, if you get my meaning."

Ming seemed ready to pop. The excitement was so much that he not only grinned, but waved his hands in giddy fashion.

"Ooooh, I have a brand new proton beam that I have been dying to test on someone. Please bring our mutual friend directly to me here."

Once the transmission ended, the dictator sat rubbing his hands as he imagined the horrors they would enjoy on the superhero. Beside him, Lotus *#13* was looking a little nervous.

Dave tried to at least pretend to be shocked by the sight of Wanda and her minion leading Mister Marvelous on a compliance chain. Each time he struggled, the length of metal would give him a painful jolt.

"Kneel before the Master." Wanda commanded the hero. When he refused to comply she poked him in the crotch with a stick. Immediately Marvelous seemed to jolt as if electricity were being transmitted through his body. A second later he collapsed to the floor on his knees. With her sword at his throat, she held him there before looking up to Ming for approval.

"My, oh my, what a *baaad* little girl you are, indeed." Ming was quite pleased with the situation.

"And such a comely young assistant as well." Nodding beside his boss, Lotus gave Callie Cadaver a wink. Immediately her face broke out in a wide grin that displayed rotting teeth littered with bits of food. A long tongue darted out of her mouth to lick her lips where the stitches had formerly been.

Picking up his camera, Dave knew it was GTFO time. He had already picked out a spot behind one of the thick ceiling columns. It would allow him good visibility, and cover from most weapons. Although he knew he was invulnerable, *it still hurt like hell whenever he was hit*.

Then, just as expected, the Supers all turned simultaneously, ripped off their flimsy disguises, and confronted Ming. A split second later, the Arches all ripped off their own disguises and confronted the Supers confronting Ming. Although it was a scene that Dave had seen in comic books many times, there was something different about actually being there. *Mostly it was a lot louder*. Really, it was deafening, with the mini-missiles detonating, and the cannon fire, shrieks & screams, all happening in a giant echo chamber.

But Ming had no intention of going easily, and the legion of troops that had been waiting in the hallway began to stream through the main doors. It was utter chaos. There were the dark brown uniforms of the guards, intermingled with flashes of light from energy weapons, accented by a shock of color as Supers tore through their ranks. From his hiding spot Dave wondered how anyone could tell what was going on down there. He reasoned that the soldiers were so thick that a hero could just swing wildly and hit someone in every direction. Really, it was like a flood of soldiers.

Like modern Spartans, the Supers killed so many soldiers that they had begun to form a wall of dead bodies, causing the incoming hoard to have to climb uphill to their deaths. On the other side of the fray, Ming fired hand-blasts at anyone who got too close. The red energy globs seemed to have a stunning effect as anyone they contacted suddenly lost all muscle control. Captain Chaos was just feet away from getting his hands on the dictator when a crimson ball of energy sent him crashing into the column where Dave hid.

"Dood!" Dave recoiled at the sight of Chaos lying unconscious in a heap. "Geez, I hope he's not really dead this time. That would be terribly ironic. But the real question is; would we still need to have another funeral, or is there a one-per week limit? Inquiring minds wanna know."

As much as he wanted to begin his own plan, Dave knew to wait for the right moment. With Ming, there would be a pitched battle, then just when he was about to suffer defeat he would pull out his ultimate weapon and capture them all en masse. After that would come the monologuing. *No Arch-Nemesis was ever complete without an afternoon of revealing their master plan.*

So Dave waited patiently, enjoying the melee. The Supers had managed to wall off the main entrance with a combination of dead bodies and Omega Girl's force field. After that the minions in the room were quickly incapacitated; Filthy Joe being the last to fall. Now it was just Ming and his chief minion against two dozen Supers.

Immediately the heroes moved on Ming and Lotus, but they had not gone more than a few steps before the dictator held up a little blue marble between his thumb and index finger. It seemed like an innocuous little thing to use in the face of such overwhelming power and fury. Just an itty, bitty, marble, against two dozen of the best super heroes in the entire galaxy.

Releasing the little sparkly orb, he simply smiled before giving a satisfied sign. *This was it, this was Ming's opus, the big kahuna, the latest tech toy guaranteed to incapacitate even the strongest of heroes.*

Dave knew to get the hell down as soon as he saw the harmless little marble floating through the air towards StarFire and the others. It was always that way; Ming loved to make his weapons appear inoffensive, even harmless. But then they would turn out to be insanely powerful. Dave knew this from seeing it time and again in comics. It was a recurring theme with the dictator, yet the Supers never seemed to see it coming.

Then just as Dave suspected it would, the little blue marble erupted outwards in a burst of pure plasma. But rather than burning them, the material seemed to attach itself to each of the armored heroes.

"What the…" StarFire struggled inside of her battle suit. Then a split second later they were all thrown against the outer wall with enough force to dent the metal bulkhead.

"I call this one the Gravitron." Pleased with himself, Ming stepped out into the middle of them to begin his monologue. He had so much villainy to reveal before he killed them all.

"Surely you all remember that intriguing ride in the amusement park? The Gravitron; where you are pressed to the walls by centrifugal force. Well, as you may have guessed, I was able to encapsulate that into a small, convenient package."

Looking around, Dave cautiously emerged from his hiding place. Camera in hand, it was really just a ruse. The camera had taken a direct hit from Captain Fantastic's minigun. Concealing the damage with his hand, Dave still used it as a prop to get in closer. Pretending to film each of the heroes pinned to the wall in agony, he was sure to give Ming his face-time as well.

Then without warning he acted.

"Red pill for you, blue pill for you!" Dave actually sounded cheery as he slapped a red zombie-button on the back of Ming's neck. A split second later he attached the blue button to Lotus. He had assigned the colors based on their attire, no other reason. Ming wore crimson robes so he got the red zombie button, and Lotus got the blue button by default.

No bigger than a bottle cap, the zombie buttons immediately affixed themselves to their victim by means of three little legs that dug into their flesh. It was disconcerting for Dave to watch it happen. He had seen it done in comic books, but to see it for real was actually quite creepy.

"Ewww." His mouth made a grimace. Within a second Ming was standing stiff as a board. Gritting his teeth, it was obvious the man was fighting the device with everything he had.

But Lotus had begun to convulse. Slowly at first, but increasing steadily, it was as if he were experiencing a standing seizure. Across the room Mister Marvelous was shaking his head frantically as he tried to say something. But the gravitational forces were just too much for him to utter much more than "Bluesmakeyougobluey!"

The greasy-haired minion's oscillations became quite stark as he seemed to be suffering a *grand mal* seizure while still upright. Then without warning his head exploded in a bright red spray.

It was something no one expected, except maybe Mister Marvelous. Summoning all his strength he shouted out "The blue ones make you go bluey!"

"Ooooooh." Dave suddenly had an epiphany. It was a detail not well explained in graphical media. In comic books the heroes seem to throw the things about in every direction, scoring magical hits with every shot. Only now did he understand the color coding system: *red robot, blue boom, check!*

Lotus's headless body continued to stand for several seconds before the zombie field wore off. Plummeting to the ground in a gooey crash, the image had left them all stunned.

Immediately Ming turned to Dave with a murderous expression. But before he could say anything, the cameraman spoke first.

"Yeah, I know…I'll rue the day." Dave nodded calmly. He knew this playbook too well.

"No, I was going to say that you get to thaw him out." Ming was stern in his order. "It's a ton of work, and this time I'm not doing it. You can fill the bacta tank, and purge the bio-oven, format the brain, and sit through an entire Windows installation and update. I am simply not doing it this time. You break it, you buy it." His voice dripped in sarcasm at the end.

"Fine, but after we get back." Dave agreed as he herded the dictator towards the secret exit that was always just behind the throne. Sure enough, a section of the wall slid back when Ming approached. Stepping through, they left the rest of the Supers and Arches pinned to the walls.

"So may I inquire as to the nature of this abduction?" Having been deposed twice before, Ming wondered which prison he was bound for this time. He did have his favorites.

"Rumor has it that you know how to find Professor Zero." Nodding confidently, Dave was enjoying his role in this play. Wearing Excalibur beneath is plaid shirt seemed to give his step an extra bounce.

"Zero?" Ming did his best to stop walking. The zombie button overrode his legs so the most he could do was slow down a little.

"Yeah, that's why they're here today. They mean to stop this guy together, and they seem to think you are the one guy in the galaxy who knows how to find him." Dave nodded seriously.

"I hate to disappoint you, my young friend, but you did not have to go through all this expense. If I thought the League of Carnage was interested in finding Zero, then I would have sent them that way years ago." Chuckling, Ming seemed to find it all very amusing.

"What's that supposed to mean?" Dave asked before brushing a piece of Lotus's brains off of Ming's collar. "Sorry, you got some…"

"What you don't understand about Professor Zero is that finding him was never the hard part. The difficulty is that I have lost every single villain who has ever ventured into his lair." His eyes opened wide as if he were witnessing great power. "But if the LOC wants to charge in there and be torn to pieces, then I happily bid them *adieu*. His powers are immeasurable."

"We'll see about that." Dave pulled his collar down far enough to reveal the golden suit below.

"Ahhh, Excalibur. That twas always my favorite suit of Marv's. It really grabs the light and shows up well in news footage. The fabric truly showed off Clark's glutes quite well. He's a very attractive man, you know. Very photogenic, indeed." Showing his approval, Ming's face changed on a dime. "But it won't help you one iota if you venture into the lair of Professor Zero."

"Shhhh!" Dave ordered Ming as they approached the guard post in the hanger.

"Hey, guys!" Dave greeted the guards who still stood post outside of the Sexus Navis. Bottie was the supervisor on duty today, and he looked glum to be missing all the killing.

"Eeey mon. Getting' out ahead of the riff-raff?" Bottie asked with a smile before he thought of something. "Hey, de ship ain't gonna explode after'n you leave, is it?"

"Naw. We'll be back in a few hours. I gotta fix Lotus; I totally broke him." Dave pretended to be horrified by the event.

"Oh, me know. I break him once by dropping crane on him. He not totally dead, just mostly, so we make him fully dead and da boss can make new one." Sharing his own experience with the chief minion, the hulking soldier waved his roommate past the checkpoint. *After all; no one told Bottie to check people for zombie buttons.* So even though the device was plainly visible on the back of Ming's neck, with its flashing red light and all, the soldiers were oblivious. Dave had been counting on this.

Stopping at the top of the ramp, Dave elbowed Ming as he whispered something.

"Tell the big soldier to go guard D-block for the next two hours."

Ming made a strange face, but before he could object, the zombie button made him repeat the order.

"You, the big one, I want you to go guard D-block. This is an essential mission and you must not fail under any conditions. Am I clear?" The ruler's voice was shrill at the end.

"You 'de boss!" Snapping to attention, Bottie acted as if he had been handed the mission of a lifetime. "I go kill da invaders who come!"

Continuing up the ramp, Ming finally managed to get out the words.

"What in the wide world of sports was that about?"

Chuckling, Dave thought of the big, goofy, soldier that was likely sandbagging their room by now.

"He's my roomie." Dave shrugged as the doors clanged shut behind them.

"Aaaand?" Ming coaxed him.

"And in about five minutes, every Super in the galaxy is going to come down that hallway. He's a Morganeese so he'd be compelled by his very nature to stand and fight them."

"So?" Ming still seemed baffled as to why Dave would even object. "The Morganeese love nothing better than a good fight."

"That wouldn't be a fight, they'd pave right over the top of him. He's a good guy, he doesn't deserve to get slaughtered that way." Waving that off, the cameraman knew it was true. He had just watched the Supers build a cadaver wall as if they were playing with Lincoln Logs. They would not even slow down for Bottie.

"Oh, so if you were feeling so gracious and *humane*…" Ming's voice dripped of sarcasm at the end. "Why did you only send the one guard away to safety?"

Stopping, Dave frowned before answering in a subdued voice.

"I owe the other guy money."

Ming laughed aloud before slapping the young man on the back. "I believe I am beginning to like you, Mister Meadows."

"Yeeeaaah, let's just keep this platonic, because liking leads to loving, and loving leads to fucking, and you ain't fucking me." Giving the ruler a wink, Dave let him know he was funning him.

"Ooooh, my young kidnapper. You don't know what you are missing. When I'm good I'm good, but when I'm bad, I'm great." Ming put his hands on his hips and pretended to sway like Mae West.

Dave had to give that a chuckle. It was rare to see the dictator so out of character.

"Well, just so you know, if we ever did the nasty, you'd be the *bendy*. I don't do *bendy*, me a *straightee*, definitely a *straightee*."

"My Grindr username is MurderYouInTheFace99. Look me up sometime." Giving a wink, Ming went back to his usual stiff posture.

Once aboard, Dave issued commands to the robot staff. Immediately the ship broke dock and began heading away from the fleet.

"Which way?" Dave asked, hoping he would not need to resort to torture to get his answers. He knew what a black hole that was with Ming. If Wanda couldn't dig it out of the ruler, then he doubted he would fare any better. After all, his step-sister seemed to actually enjoy all of the torturing. On the video she had flailed him with the cat-o-nine-tails, then healed him, then repeated the process so many times that she started complaining of tennis elbow. *But Dave and torture? Not so much.*

"Well?" Pretending to be serious, the cameraman eyed the dictator.

Glaring at Dave for the longest moment, Ming finally relented.

"Fine, but it's your funeral. Though honestly, I doubt there will be any type of memorial service. Most likely they will simply have the custodian mop up your remains after everyone has gone home. *Cleanup on aisle five!"* Pretending to call out as if he were in a Wal-Mart, the dictator typed in the coordinates. Immediately the luxury liner jumped to hyper-zoom.

Sitting back as the stars streaked past their windows, Dave evaluated the dictator under the less formal circumstances. Finally he had to ask something that had been bugging him all morning.

"So how did you know they were going to attack? Is StarFire really a double agent?" He was sure he had this one pegged.

"Mmmm. I was CC'ed a copy of the itinerary, of course." Ming seemed surprised at the question. "StarFire an arch? That would be a true miracle, but no, she is devoted to her faction, though I believe she missed her true calling."

"Yeah, I think her and my mom got their charts switched while Zero had 'em." Tilting his head to one side, he backtracked to something Ming had said. "So they emailed you about the battle?"

"Of course." Ming failed to grasp why it would be a problem. "You simply cannot expect a battle that epic without some serious planning. I mean, I had to bring in thousands of soldiers, and find motels for all of the Arches who would be in town, and the arch union requires at least one med-bot per member so I had to place a massive order, then there were the cameras. What would be the point of the battle if the footage does not stun the senses? We don't battle for our own benefit; we battle for the bovine masses to enjoy."

"So this is all just a vanity thing for you guys?" It had started to gall him just how shallow these people seemed to be.

"I do not think you fully understand just how much these battles help me do my job and keep the peace. What you fail to take into account is that crusades like Mister Marvelous' tax plan, though highly supported in their own planetary system, are hugely unpopular elsewhere in the galaxy. If I do not tax Relcor then I must tax Boraan or SelDor. But if I do that, then I draw the ire of those planets, and no one is happy. But if I frame it as a patriotic move against the villainous dictator who rules with an iron fist, make these confrontations about *sticking it to the man*, then I gain tacit approval for the necessary legislative changes. I use that support to establish a compromise; Relcor only pays part of the tax, and the rest is pulled from enhanced projects on Boraan or SelDor."

"So it's all a sham?" Dave seemed disappointed.

"Oh, quite the contrary!" The dictator's eyes lit up as he explained further. He had missed his chance to monologue earlier so he simply had to get it out of his system. "You see, when I work with elected politicians, they barrage me with useless legislation. So many banal requests and blatant modifications to benefit their contributors. They are legislators, and that is what they are designed to do; write legislation. They are constantly inventing crisis where none exists. But with the Supers, I am dealing with just a few bullet points. They sort out the felgerkarb and come to me with a clear message. That I can respect, that I can work with. But all of the babble of those politicians, it's like being in a hen house. I have twice fed these vermin to my guards, but they only grow back. *Damned local elections.*"

Dave could see how this process could work, or really, had worked since long before he was born.

"You must understand that although I knew the time and place for the battle, there are some very serious rules governing these encounters, the host is not able to use their super weapon for at least five minutes, no nukes or other dirty weapons—we believe in green battles…" Ming was ticking things off his finger as the ship began to slow. Approaching fast in the window was an orbital platform. Roughly the size of a shopping mall, it was obvious what the place was some kind of a medical care facility.

"Professor Zero works in an UrgentCare?" Looking about as they parked in the emergency lane, Dave found it an odd place. He expected the guy who pulled Ming's strings to at least have an evil castle, or a dilapidated warehouse, but instead it was a brightly lit medical facility.

"Well, this is where he comes when he is not out kidnapping and torturing children. I have no idea what he does in there; this is as far as any of my Arches have gotten before they stopped reporting in. If you go through that door, you will die. That is not conjecture, but simple fact. Just as sure as the sky is green and water is polluted, if you poke the bear, the bear will eat you in most horrific fashion." Ming had an earnest look in his eyes. He truly believed what he was telling the young man.

"Luckily you will be there to introduce us." Smiling, Dave shoved the dictator ahead.

"You are not going to believe this, but I actually have a dental appointment on the other side of the galaxy in ten minutes, so I'll just duck out, if that's okay." The ruler had managed to make a u-turn before Dave grabbed him by his ornate collar and hauled him along.

"Nice try, but I happen to know that Captain Collider knocked out all of your teeth at the battle of Pythar, and your new teeth are made out of zirconium. Literally, your teeth are as hard as diamonds." Dave was not falling for it.

"That's not entirely true." Ming held up a finger as he protested. "I did lose a crown at the battle of Pythar, but the whole story about diamond teeth was just propaganda that

Lotus came up with. He reads all of those *ridiculous* comic books." Ming rolled his eyes at the last part. Trying to seem brave, the dictator was keenly aware of the very real danger that awaited him inside. He only hoped the professor would understand that he had no part of this. He could still remember the sight of Hugh G Member, impaled on the Dubai towers that morn. The way he had silhouetted at sunrise, it had completely disrupted morning prayers. At the time Ming had seen it for what it was: a warning to all Supers and Arches to stay in line.

Stopping in front of the directory, Dave scanned the rows of names listed there but saw no sign of Professor Zero. Elbowing his prisoner, he was met with a shrug.

"I have no idea." Ming admitted. "I told you that everyone who gets past those doors ends up dead, and we are *decidedly* past those doors."

"Humph." Dave gave a satisfied grunt. "There he is: Doctor Eugene Nome."

"Eh?" Doctor Gene Nome, genome." Ming cackled at the pun. "Good, now you just have to get us past his nurse, Tiny."

Dave saw the nameplate on the desk first. He almost laughed aloud at the name. After that his eyes panned upwards, and kept panning, and panning until his head was tilted back. Only then did he get to the top of the massive, bald man that was parked behind the comically small desk. He had been so big that Dave's eyes had originally thought him part of the background. He estimated Nurse Tiny would have been fifteen feet tall were he to stand up. *Incredible!*

"Do you have an appointment?" The squeaky voice that came out of Nurse Tiny's mouth was comical.

"Oh, hi, Nurse Thanos, is it?" Dave kidded before turning serious. "Actually I have a billing question, I got this in the mail the other day." Dave pretended to pull something out of his pocket as he stood before the desk. Curious, Tiny leaned over to see what it was.

But instead, the only thing the cameraman pulled out of his pocket was a fist. Swinging with all his might, he could feel Excalibur spring to life under his clothes. With the power of a wrecking ball, his fist made contact with the nurse's square chin.

The impact was surprisingly loud. **POW!** He could only imagine how loud it must have been inside of Nurse Tiny's head. The punch was so powerful that it drove the man up through the ceiling and out into space.

"Pow, zoom, to the moon, baby!" The young cameraman chuckled as he looked through the gaping hole in the ceiling. In the distance the giant was flapping his arms and legs uselessly.

"C'mon. Introduce me to your guy." Shoving Ming, Dave was adamant.

"He will never give in to your plans to dismantle his network. You should turn back now." Ming warned.

"No, you don't get it. THEY want to dismantle the network." Gesturing over his shoulder Dave indicated the supers they had left behind. "I just want my mom released from her faction before the Divas in spandex get here and screw everything up. That's it. You self-entitled buncha *prima donnas* can battle each other till the cows come home for all I care. I just want my Mom out."

"Then you may want to accelerate your plan." Ming said as he looked over his shoulder. "Because *they* seem to have caught up with us."

Dave glanced back, then did a double take when he saw the *Mons Machina* casting a shadow over the entire facility.

"How the hell did they catch up so fast?" Dave was surprised at the sight of dozens of ships dropping out of FTL.

"The Red Reaper drives for Uber in his spare time, so he knows all the shortcuts." Ming observed with a nod.

"One of your captains drives for Uber?" Dave's face showed scorn.

"Oh yes, he has a solid five star rating." Ming seemed quite proud of that fact.

"Dood, you seriously need to pay your henchmen better."

Shaking it off, Dave hustled through the doors only to find himself in a nondescript lab. Nothing special really, just some tables, a few beakers, and a long row of human-shaped morphing chambers. The sight of the genetic booths chilled him as he saw the myriad of needles that would be plunged into whoever was unlucky enough to find themselves strapped into the thing.

For his own part, Ming seemed to get the *heebie-jeebies* from the sight of the morphing chambers. No doubt he remembered his own time in the booths.

Looking around, Dave could see a man in a lab coat seated at a desk in the corner. Scribbling furiously in a notepad, he didn't notice them right away. Finally looking up, the scientist seemed irritated to see them there.

"This is a restricted area, you'se guys needs to leave." Rising, he revealed himself to be a fat little man, with a scruffy beard and thick glasses. The polyester tie he wore appeared to be a clip-on.

"Introduce us." Dave squoze Ming's shoulder.

"This is Dave. He's Raven's son, and you should know that I am here against my will." Giving a perfunctory smile when he was done, Ming stepped to the back of the conversation. When the killing started, he wanted to be far away. He had survived this long by knowing when to fight, and when to run like hell. *And this was time for the latter*.

"You got a lotta balls comin' to my lab." The Professor's voice had a distinct Jersey accent to it. "Normally I just kill assholes who come here, but sometimes I gets curious about why they'd come here, against better judgment. Y'know what I mean? So before I turn you into a pile of dust and have the

Roomba sweep you up, tell me what it is that you felt was so important as to be worth coming here and risking your balls for all eternity? Enlighten me."

Coming close, the fat little man turned his head so his ear was facing Dave. Despite being a head shorter than the cameraman, the Professor seemed intent on invading his personal space aggressively.

"I want my mother released from the evil faction so she can work wherever she wants." Standing his ground, he suspected that any sign of weakness would earn him a refusal.

"Ummm, lemme think about that." Pretending to give it consideration for all of two seconds, Zero was clearly mocking the young man "No. N-o. Nope, not gonna happen. No dice, snake-eyes, f'get about it!" Still standing practically on Dave's toes, the Professor was not subtle as he challenged the photojournalist.

Dave had already invested plenty of time in working out this scenario. He had always planned on appealing to the man's maternal instincts, but if that failed there would only be one option.

"If there is no way that I can appeal to you to free her from the evil faction, then I'd have no choice but to remove you from the process." Grabbing the scientist by the collar, Dave pulled a tennis-ball sized orb from his pocket. At the same time his clothes began to glow and burn bright before being incinerated away. Within just a few seconds, he was standing there in the golden suit Excalibur.

Zero took a sharp breath as he felt himself being picked up off the floor by the iron grip of Excalibur. Glancing down he could see the thermal detonator in Dave's hands. First he wondered where in hell Dave had even found the thing, then he wondered where the cameraman intended to **put** it.

"Free her or I shove this thing up your *dookie-chute* and pull the pin." The cameraman made it clear he would shove the grenade in to his elbow. "That's all I'm asking for, free my Mom so she can be a nurse or a hero or whatever she wants to be. You were an asshole to make her a villain and make StarFire a heroine. Total dick-move."

There was a look of terror on Zero's face as his stubby little legs seem to run in mid air. Panicked, it almost looked like he would stroke out there for a moment. Then abruptly his terror turned to laughter.

It was not a casual laugh, or a snicker; it was a full-belly roar. As if he were laughing at a joke, the professor showed no fear whatsoever. Although this confused Dave, one thing was clear: Zero was not laughing **with** him.

"Your type are all the same. Without your powers you're nothing but pussies." No sooner had he said it than a white flash of energy emanated out from the little scientist. Washing over Dave, he felt himself stagger a little as he dropped Zero.

Stumbling a few paces, Dave could feel the heaviness of his suit. Right away he could tell that there was something wrong with Excalibur.

"You broke my suit." Dave was aghast. "Now you're definitely getting a grenade up the *dookie-chute*."

"Unlikely. Without your super powers, you ain't nuthin but another dumb-ass civilian." Reaching into his pocket, Zero pulled a small pistol. Smiling briefly he bid adieu. "Goodbye Mister...y'know, I don't even know your name?"

The gun flashed, the slide operated, and the projectile spat out the muzzle, all in a nanosecond. Striking Dave center-mass, it was a perfect heart-shot as it impacted just under the sternum. Zero's smile returned as the scientist took joy in scrutinizing his enemy's face.

"I always enjoy watching a man's expression as they die. I truly relish that moment, when they have that final epiphany that they are really about to die. I enjoy that look so much." His beady eyes flicked back and forth between Dave's eyes, as if he expected them to do something special. "Yessss, show me."

Dave felt the pain, it was such a sharp stabbing sensation, so unlike the energy weapons he had been hit with thus far. He was actually quite surprised how much bullets hurt. But then something curious happened; the pain began to subside. Looking down he was shocked to see no injury at all.

"But I took your powers with that Tetrionic blast just now, you should a civilian now...?" Zero's voice spoke of his surprise.

"You didn't give me my powers, so you can't take 'em." Dave smiled. "Now it's time for you to pay for the suit."

"No, wait!" Trying to use the gun again, the professor was shocked when Dave slapped it out of his hands. Punching him across the face, the cameraman intended to flip him around for the insertion.

"Pucker up, bitch." It felt odd to say the words; he had always been the good boy. Yet by the same token he felt justified by the matronly nature of his mission; he was literally on a quest for his mother. Besides, he felt no remorse for anything that happened to the man who had been playing puppet master with an entire galaxy for half a century. On a more personal basis, Dave's entire life had been a series of potholes and roadblocks, all thanks to the tubby little tyrant before him. A thermal detonator would give him just the warm-fuzzy feeling that he deserved.

Dave was about to yank the man's pants down when the fat little scientist spun around surprisingly fast. Swinging his arm, he caught Dave across the side of the head with enough force to throw him bodily across the room. Blinking his eyes, the cameraman saw more stars than the constellation Andromeda. *That punch had been epic.*

Sitting up, this time it was Dave who felt himself being grabbed by the collar and yanked into the air.

The young photojournalist only had time to realize that it was Professor Zero who was lifting him off the ground by his neck. Trying to struggle, Dave quickly found that his grip was even stronger than StarFire's.

"So," Zero opened up with a grin on his scruffy little face. "Even though you'se knew that I was going around the galaxy, giving out super powers likes there was no tomorrow, it never occurred to you that I may have kept the very best stuff for myself? Eh?"

Flashing yellow teeth at Dave, the professor next slammed the cameraman against the floor several times before launching him into a far wall with enough force to leave a Dave-shaped dent in the metal bulkhead.

Landing with a thud, he vaguely realized he was lying practically at Ming's feet in the back of the room. Someone tall and bald looked down at the young photojournalist before making a clucking sound.

"I believe this is the part where I reference previous conversations by pointing out that *I told you so!*"

Dave groaned before casting the elderly dictator an evil eye of his own. "You could help, y'know."

"I was honestly considering that…" Ming pretended as if he had truly labored over the decision. "But it has been my observation that people are typically much happier in life when their skull remains attached to their body."

"But I'm invulnerable." Dave tried to comfort himself with that thought as he got to his hands and knees.

"And how will that work when he rips you into fifty little pieces?" Ming pretended to scratch his chin as if deep in thought.

Dave never had a chance to consider that as Zero's iron grip closed on his ankle like a steel bear trap. A split second later the cameraman felt himself being flailed back and forth against the floor. The pain was excruciating as he never even had time to reset before he was again slamming into the marble tile. He had lost count of how many times he had cracked his skull.

Head spinning, Dave felt himself tossed into the far corner of the room. Using his face to soften the landing, he collapsed in a heap.

The big doors into the room slammed open, framing StarFire, Marvelous, Wanda, and dozens more. Like great Spartans of old they looked magnificent as their image filled the doorway. Then slowly the double doors began to rebound closed right in their faces, ruining their epic entry.

While Dave wanted to take a moment and laugh at the comedy of how their big moment was interrupted, he knew what was coming next, and he wanted to get out of the way before it happened.

On his hands and knees, he did his best to crawl to one side of the room. A split second later StarFire's crimson energy cannon blew both the main doors across the room in a blinding flash. Not pausing a second, the heroes began rushing through the breach.

"You'se guys has some great timing!" Zero seemed entirely pleased to find the entire horde of Supers and Arches standing there before him. He doubted there were more than a few missing, making this the perfect opportunity to drive home his point, once and for all. "Please, come in, all of you'se. There's plenty of room. Yes, yes, we can fit all of you'se in here."

Clasping his hands, the tubby little professor stood in the middle of the room as they filed in around him. While the Arches and Heroes had once been enemies, today they stood united against the man who had victimized them all so many years ago.

Still trying to untangle himself in the corner, Dave wanted to tell them to run away, that he was about to take their powers with one of his energy blasts, but he was still winded from the thrashing. It was like getting gut-punched fifty times, then hit by a speeding train. All that would come out of the cameraman's mouth was a bit of wheezing.

Across the room, Ming had been the only one with enough sense to get out before it was too late. Nearly to the exit, it was Wanda who grabbed him before he quite reached the threshold.

"Not so fast!" Dragging him back, she felt that she safely spoke for both factions in this.

"I left my inhaler in the ship." Ming made a patently false claim.

"Then you'll just have to suck it up." Smiling cruelly, Wanda shoved the dictator back into the front lines.

"Good, you'se all here. Very excellent. Okay, first lemme open up by saying that I thought it very brave that you'se would all come out here to see me wit' your concerns. That took guts, that took real chutzpah. I commends ya' for it. But it's gotta stop. I got lots of work to do, and for every one of you'se that I gotta kill, I gotta go find some young kid and turn 'em into the heroing machine that each of you are. So really it's just better if you all stop coming here...forever." Still smiling as if he were proud of them, it was a thin veneer. The deception could be seen in the way he only smiled with his mouth. His eyes told a much different story.

"We'll never come back if you meet our demands." Wanda put some gravel in her voice.

"Is this the part where you expect me to show some kinda interest in yer demands? Maybe talk it out wit' ya a little? Eh?" He raised an eyebrow as the smile abruptly vanished. "Allow me to counter-offer."

Snapping his fingers, the Professor activated filaments that were built into the floor. Immediately the Supers and Arches felt themselves being held in place by pure energy coursing through their bodies. The sensation was agonizing, as if all of their muscles were cramping up in Charlie-horses at the same time. That is, all but Dave, who still lay in a pile by the eyewash station. Moving slowly now, he seemed to be untangling his limbs. The cameraman had not gone far when he was again yanked to his feet by the collar. Looking up, Dave found he was being held out for all to see as the professor launched into his monologue.

"So now for your collective *ed-if-ication*, I will now demonstrate what will happen to every one of you'se Supers and Arches that gets within a parsec of this office. Each of you may be proud of your tiny-little smattering of abilities, but I have put together my own amazing portfolio of powers. I can literally shoot fire out of my ass. But that's not what we're gonna see here today. Nope. Here is how things is gonna work from now on; I'm gonna give you chumps a last warning to stay the hell away, then I'm gonna rip this young man into pieces as an example, then all of you'se are gonna go back to your lives and do whatever the hell I tells you to do. *Capice*?"

Held in place by his electronic bindings, Ming could only shake his head sadly. "I get so tired of being right all of the time."

"So before I start the ripping, I'd just like to let you'se all know that we, the organization, we do really appreciate your efforts. It means a lot to us, really."

For Dave there had never been a worse moment in his life. He had completely misjudged the situation, thought that his clever idea would actually work. He had simply not expected the Professor to be so damned strong. But it was true; Ming had warned him against this very thing, and now here he was…about to be torn apart in front of dozens of people, merely to set an example. As if that were not the worst; his invulnerability powers would keep him alive for every bit of it. Behind him he could hear Zero monologuing about how important it was for them to do their jobs, how the very fabric of the universe depended on them doing their jobs, and how they must obey the three rules for the sake of all existence. It all sounded like drivel he had read a thousand times in comic books. All those years of reading those stupid comics he had always envisioned himself the hero. Never had he imagined he would be the waif who gets murdered on page three.

He knew that his life would end when Zero finished monologuing. This he knew with absolute certainty. Struggle as he might, there was nothing he could do against the professor's incredible strength. Looking up he tried to at least take solace in the fact that for one brief moment, he was a Super; he had been one of those costumed faces that now witnessed his demise. That was worth something wasn't it? To be a Super, even if for just a day, was better than a lifetime of obscurity. He truly felt this in his heart. But the feeling evaporated as he could feel himself being flipped around for what was to be the beginning of his end.

Now facing Zero, he could smell the man's onion breath, and still see the hotdog bun lodged in his crooked teeth. He was a revolting little slob of a man.

"I got just one question." Dave panted out the words.

"Oooh, a last, dying question. I do enjoy those." Zero's casual laugh told the room that he was not posturing; he truly enjoyed this part. Not that it came as a surprise to any of the mutant witnesses; they had all spent days under his cruel hands. None of them doubted the sadistic glee of Professor Zero.

"All those powers you gave yourself…was one of them invulnerability?" Dave croaked out the question a split second before they heard the shot.

Zero's face took a sudden change of course, switching from glee to surprise. Looking down he could see his own gun in Dave's hands. Panning down further, he saw a growing red spot on his own white shirt. His mouth moved but nothing came out.

Dave was dropped to the ground, gun in hand. Catching his breath he watched the grubby little scientist stagger backwards as he realized he only had seconds to live. The shot had been center mass, shattering his heart. It was only due to the small caliber of the pistol that he was alive at all. The little .380 bullet had come to rest inside of the left ventricle of his heart, allowing vital fluid to be ejected with each pump.

"No…nooo, the galaxy will collapse…without…you have to…help him! He's our only hope…" Gripping something around his neck, Professor Zero seemed to be trying to give it to Dave as he collapsed to the floor dead. Immediately the security field released the rest of the Supers and Arches from their painful confinement.

"By Grapthar's Hammer, what agony that be!" Captain Archimedes shook his head. It had been sheer anguish the way the energy coursed up one leg, then across the pelvis, and back down the other leg, like a detour of pure pain. It felt like he had been raped with a bolt of lightning.

"I didn't mind it really." Ming shrugged before rubbing his crotch. "I'm hard as a rock."

"TMI." Wanda commented as she used her hand to shove Ming's face out of her path. "What's this thing he was trying to give you?"

"I dunno." Dave had made his way over to the Professor's dead body. On a gold chain around his neck was a curious thing. "I think it's a key, but I've never seen a lock like this would fit."

Holding up the key, they could all see that it was just a flat piece of card stock, cut to a curious shape. There was some looking about by the mutants in the room before an Arch in the back spoke up.

"There's a skinny little slot on the wall over here." The horned beast seemed to find the spot suspicious.

Moving forward, Dave inserted the key. No sooner had it slid into battery than they heard a clicking sound that seemed to emanate through the floor and walls. Everyone in the room gave a little start at that; it was as if he had triggered a massive change somewhere in the station.

"I should probably go warm up the escape ship." Ming tried to make a dash for the door, only to be blocked by his own people. "Or I could stay here with all of you and be incinerated."

Stepping back, Dave left the key in the lock as the wall around it began to glisten and shine. Then slowly it faded until there was no wall at all. This amazed the cameraman; he had never seen this type of technology. In his world doors were always mechanical things that opened with loud whooshing sounds. But to see a door that operated by melting away before their eyes, that caught their attention immediately.

But it was what lay beyond the portal that gave them a jolt.

The room was large, even bigger than the laboratory had been. In his mind this detail spoke to Dave. Having seen the building from the outside, he knew that the professor's lab had been on the far north side of the complex, the last lab before you were outside of the building. So if there was another room still, it meant the laboratory was somehow bigger on the inside than it was on the outside. By their laws of physics that was impossible, yet here he was looking at exactly that phenomenon right now. Where there should have been the vacuum of space was an entire alien habitat.

As if the architecture of the room wasn't enough to convince them this place had not been built by humans, the bedridden alien in the corner confirmed it. There, laboring to breathe, was the creature. Long and slender, with deep black eyes, the being looked as if it could have hailed from some distant human ancestry, millions of years ago. Blinking its black orbs, it beckoned them weakly.

While Dave's attention was fully enveloped by the sight of the alien, he was slowly becoming aware of the other things around it. There was medical equipment, and intravenous dispensers, and other unidentifiable devices, all clearly of alien design. While he was unsure what most of it did, he surmised that the being was dying.

Behind him the rest of the Supers and Arches spread out as they examined the curious items in the room. There were so many devices, but even the simplest of them defied their understanding. More astounding yet was that none of the equipment had any buttons or knobs or external controls. The more they examined, the more they became convinced that this creature was genuinely not from their galaxy.

With his sister standing beside him, Dave slowly approached the hospital bed. Holding up a hand, he wanted the being to know he came in peace. Stopping at the foot of the bed he could see that the alien's veins seemed to pulse as it labored to breathe.

"What is all of this?" Wanda kept her voice level as she gestured to the room.

"This is my home." The words resonated in their heads, spoken so clear that there was no mistaking it. "I am proud to see my children have made it back to their origins. I had hoped to see this day before my time ended for all eternity."

"Why did you make us fight like gladiators in a ring?" Wanda's tone was a little harsh. Dave put a hand on her shoulder to rein her in.

"She's not wrong; we have a right to know why you chose us, why you forced us to be loyal to a faction? These were our lives you were playing with here. We have a right to know why." His eyes furrowed with concern, Dave felt sympathy for the being that lay dying before him. As he stood there he could feel flashes of images and sensations from the alien. Already he knew it was very old, and it felt a great regret for something it had done.

"I never wanted to hurt any of you; I only wanted to repair the damage I had done to your reality." There was true sincerity to the voice in their heads. Along with the words they could feel waves of remorse for the great sin it had committed.

"What damage?" Dave could see the images, but none of it made sense to him. They seemed to be pictures from an unfamiliar world.

"I am a being from another dimension, much unlike your corporeal existence. During my careless travels I passed through your galaxy and shattered it."

Again they could feel more flashes of terror as an entire galaxy screamed in unison. Throughout all of it they could feel the alien's dread at realizing what it had done.

"But our galaxy was never destroyed, or we wouldn't be here?" Dave pointed out hesitantly, still unsure how these images fit into their history.

"No…" Came the booming voice in their heads. "The fabric of your world was never compromised. It was your reality that I shattered. Your entire perception of right and wrong, good and bad, these were just a few of the reference datum that I had completely obliterated in my moment of haste."

"The dark ages…" Ming trailed off as he remembered studying the era. Things had been utterly chaotic in those days. It had been a different galaxy before the mutants.

"But there was a problem…" The voice in their head changed to a concerned tone. "For although I possessed the power to put you back together, you are the only corporeal beings I have ever encountered and I had no idea what your world should look like. I did the best I could, but the only model I had to go by was the sacred library. It was all I had rescued from your old world before I broke it irreparably."

With a shaky finger, the being pointed to the bookshelf in the far corner. It was the only recognizable thing in the room. There was another device as well, a box with two big, round wheels and a tape stretching between them and through the box. Dave noticed the power switch on the side of the device, but resisted the urge to touch it until he knew more. Advancing towards the book shelf, the rest of the Supers opened a hole for him to pass through. Plucking a rectangular box from the shelf, the cameraman raised an eyebrow as he read the label.

"What is a Star War?" Dave asked aloud. "How do stars have war?"

Continuing down the shelf he listed the ones that piqued his interest. "*Wizard of Oz, Lord of the Rings, BattleStar, Avengers, X-Men, Seven Samurai, The Magnificent Seven*...those last two sound oddly derivative? What are these?" Pulling the video tapes out of their boxes, he had never seen such odd technology.

Unlike her brother, Wanda felt no hesitation to see what the switch by the box did. Flipping it, she jumped when it cast a bright box of light on Mister Marvelous.

Sure that the light was somehow toxic or a death ray, Marv gave a squeal before jumping out of the way.

But the box of light turned out to be some kind of a video, projected on the far wall. There was a tinny sound from the box as it played. All around the camera Ming and the others made *ooh* and *ahh* sounds as they watched the reels slowly turn, sending film from one reel to the other in a process that was positively magical to them. *Normally they watched things like this on crappy little viewport screens.*

First there was music, followed by words appearing in the middle of the picture.

"Flash Gordon?" Ming laughed aloud? "What comical theater this is. Why, I bet the villain is some pasty-skinned hack who could not act his way out of a paper sack if you drew him a dotted line."

Everyone stopped and looked at the dictator as he stood there in his flowing gown and rubbing his hands maniacally. Just a few feet away, projected on the screen, stood a skinny villain with a shaved head, wearing a flowing gown and rubbing his hands maniacally. The resemblance was uncanny.

"What is this…?" Dave was unsure. Some of the blurbs on the back of the films sounded suspiciously like their own reality.

"It was the only model of your universe I had to go by. Each of you were created to establish and perpetuate the concepts of good and evil in your culture. Your people need to have both far extremes to help them find their way down the middle. Without your beacons, they would be lost in the night. It is for this reason that you must continue your work; for the sake of your universe."

As the alien spoke, they could see so many things in their own minds. It was like a waterfall of images and sensations. Clearly the alien was *far* advanced to them. Even its casual thoughts were Nobel Prize material in their world. It was staggering the things they could see through its eyes.

"It's so clear now, why it had to be." Dave was nodding as he truly felt the alien's pain. Even as it faced its own mortality, it harbored a deep desire to honor a debt it owed them. Probing deeper, the cameraman could even detect a strong vein of humiliation over the grievous wrong it had committed all those years ago.

Then, something changed in the images they were seeing. No longer the dark and desperate world they had been seeing, now they could see a bright new sunrise over Hopus IV. The scene was breathtaking in its promise for a new beginning. Slowly they began to see how their model would be the pattern for a great new world to come.

"But I cannot continue the fight with you, my time has come…to [cough] hand over the key to humanity's [gasp] future." Holding out a shaking fist, the alien's fingers opened to reveal a small gleaming key. In their minds they could feel the mood music as it swept their emotions up into a powerful wave. Every Super and Arch in the room held their breath as Dave reached out for that shining key that promised prosperity and good for all…

Well, all of them except Wanda, who had been suspicious from the start. After years of hunting for Professor Zero, she had seen that goal as the end-all mission of her career. End Zero and end the evil puppet master. But to learn that it was really all a construct to save humanity seemed to stick in her craw for some reason. It was too perfect, tied up with such a pretty bow. In her experience, nothing was ever neat and tidy.

The sound of mini-rockets screeching out of her arm caused everyone in the room to jump with surprise. Impacting the bedridden alien in rapid succession, the salvo of 30 explosive-tipped missiles reduced the alien to a green slurry that splashed everywhere. *But mostly on Dave.*

Still bent over with his hand held out to accept the key, he had been so surprised by the mini-missiles that his jaw had dropped open, only to have alien goo splashed into his mouth.

"Ooooohhh! Geez." Spitting and trying to wipe the *spooge* off his face, Dave turned to his sister. "What the frack was that? Now how am I supposed to save the frickin' galaxy?"

Ignoring her brother's rage, she scooped up the key from a puddle of blood.

"The mission is all a trick. It's just a new carrot for you to spend your life chasing." She scowled before showing the key. "But this is a test to see if one among us can rise up above the others, to see beyond the farcical game they have trapped us in."

Tossing the key to the ground, she used her finger disintegrators to destroy the thing. When she was done blasting, there was nothing but a dark smudge where the mysterious key had been.

"Or you just damned the galaxy." Dave was angry. He preferred the days before he even knew he had a sister.

"No, there's more than we are seeing." She nodded as her eyes began looking for the hidden camera. "The alien was just a distraction, wasn't it? We're still being tested, aren't we?"

There were some murmurs around the room as the other mutants exchanged opinions. Most were of a mind that she should have found out what the key unlocked before destroying it. Others thought she was right; the story had been quite suspicious.

"NO MORE GAMES! TALK TO US!" Using her super voice, Wanda commanded the ceiling as if there was someone there. Like her brother, she had also noticed that this room seemed to exist in another dimension than the medical office they had originally entered. Either someone had rewritten the very laws of physics, or their reality was still being toyed with.

Gritting her teeth, Wanda stood firm as she awaited a response. Convinced that they were still being played, she would settle for nothing less than the truth. The silence in the room had begun to grow awkward before something happened.

It was the bright white light that captivated them all. Streaming down from the sky where Wanda had shouted her demands, the rays seemed to glimmer like the sun. Yet despite the unfathomable intensity, it did not hurt their eyes to stare at it. In fact, the light was the most beautiful thing they had ever seen in their existence. Eager to see it with her own eyes, Wanda stripped off her wig and mask before dropping them to the floor. With her golden curls spilling out across her shoulders, she stepped forward angelically towards the light.

"Is it…you…God?" Polly felt almost breathless in her anticipation. In her mind she could feel so much more than the simple images and clips the alien had broadcast. The sensory waves that bathed her now were true emotions that filled her very soul. All around her the other mutants were slowly converging on the light as they too felt it.

Several even dropped to their knees in prayer.

"It's really him, it's the god of NetFlix!" Captain Chaos sputtered the words as he staggered along like a lemming. His concussion had left him a little loopy.

Booming out, the voice soothed them as it spoke. "All of you have fulfilled your duties with honor and distinction. Your blood and sweat have been the inspiration and guidance for the entire galaxy."

There was several seconds of basking in God's eternal light. It felt so warm and perfect, like a cat in a window sill. Each of them; Ming, Wanda, Marv, StarFire, and even concussed Captain Chaos, all knew without a doubt that they were now in the presence of their one and only maker. *They were talking to God.*

"For your selfless servitude and diligence, each of you will be awarded the mark of the Eternal One; a sign of respect and authority throughout the galaxy, for you have risen above all others of your kind and proven yourselves worthy." As God spoke in their heads, they each found a beautiful pendant appearing on their uniform. Clearly a decoration, the medal seemed to call out to anyone who laid eyes on it. Golden hue for heroes, and bright crimson red for villains.

"We are but humble servants!" Ming was on his knees right away, blubbering his loyalty to the deity.

"Good, it is very good, for I need each of you to continue the fight, continue to lead and inspire the people of the Milky Way Galaxy. From this day henceforth and herewith all of you shall be known as the Chosen Ones, and you shall be revered among all others."

There was the sound of angels singing in the sky above them. Looking around, Dave noticed that the alien's bedroom was gone now, replaced by ethereal clouds. Looking at the others around him, they had all begun kneeling and bowing. While the light above warmed his soul, there was something about it all that didn't sit right with him. He could not quite put his finger on it, but something just did not add up in his mind. Having met a goodly number of heroes and villains, he had not found that any of them were particularly nice people, even the Supers. The best of them were vain, self-centered, and egocentric. To have God himself heap such praise on them seemed inconsistent with his way of thinking. At minimum, it represented a fairly low bar to divinity. Even his philandering father was now suddenly a righteous man? Hell, for that matter, Ming was too. *In what version of the multiverse was Ming a good guy?*

"If you were really God, then I wouldn't be able to do this." Pulling his last thermal detonator from where it hung on his utility belt, he flicked off the safety and tossed the thing into the light.

"Noooo!" Polly shouted out a second before the device detonated.

Normally the thermal detonator would have turned anything in the room to pure plasma, but today something different happened. As the Thorium ignited at the molecular level, their entire world was shattered. Looking around in those nanoseconds, Dave was surprised to see his existence breaking into pieces like a mirror. Glancing down, he gulped anxiously as one of the cracks ran right through his waist. Then came another crack, and another. As their reality shattered into an infinite number of pieces, they felt themselves falling in a mess of glass and debris. *Falling, shattering…*

In the darkness they fell for what seemed like an eternity. Really there was no way to gauge time in that inky blackness. It could have been a minute, or it could have been an eon. All they knew was that when they saw the light again, it was far below them and rushing upwards fast. Sucking in his breath, Dave tried to brace for the impact. They were falling so fast, and the ground was approaching…

Then with the pain of a thousand punches, he hit the floor with a thud. Actually there were two thuds as he bounced on impact. It almost felt as if the impact had flattened one side of his face. Raising his head up the tiniest bit he was just about to exclaim joy when Wanda landed on his back.

"Ooooof!" He made a woofing sound as the air was blasted out of him by her fall.

"Ouch!" Polly screamed at the pain of landing in a seated position, oblivious to the fact that she just used her brother as a landing pad.

Dave had only just realized what had happened when yet another body landed on top of Polly, who was still on top of him.

"Ooow!" Shouted the woman in leather.

"OOF!" Came the sound from Dave on the bottom. He saw a splash of red robes and realized that it was Ming who had landed on top of them all.

"He's heavier than he looks!" Dave cursed in his mind as he tried to catch his breath.

They heard Marvelous land a few feet away, and then there were the sounds of other voices as they seemed to miss the room and keep falling. After a few seconds their cries faded away.

Standing up, Dave was happy that he was intact. After hitting the ground at terminal velocity, he would have expected to at least be in more pain, yet he felt quite chipper.

"You killed God!" Polly's voice was shrill. "Really, now God is dead. Congratulations."

"Well, now him and Nietzsche have something to talk about." Dave laughed it off. "What is this place, anyhow?"

"A library of some sort…" Marvelous had made a 180 degree turn of the room before he stopped with his mouth agape.

Like the others, Ming and Polly both scanned the room slowly, taking in as many details as they could. But once they reached the same azimuth as Marvelous, they too stood with their mouths open in surprise.

Polly had never seen such a person; his skin was black, with a sheen to it. He had a broader nose as well, centered just below those stern eyes. Shaved head and coal-black eyes only made him stand out all the more. Dressed in a fine suit, he looked unlike anything she had ever imagined.

Dave nearly jumped out of his skin when he saw the black man sitting there clapping his hands slowly in mock celebration. While he felt drawn to the man's eyes, especially the way they seemed to almost bore through him, it was the words floating just a few inches off the ground that really grabbed Dave's attention. It puzzled him how the letters seemed to be painted in midair that way.

"Samuel L. Jackson; Thespian, and Beloved Celebrity." Ming read the floating caption

In his chair, the man in the fine suit had tapered off his clapping as he now sat glaring at the quartet.

"Where are we?" Dave asked as he looked over the man for clues.

"And who the hell are you?" Marvelous tried to keep his disgust to himself. But the black man in the chair was so unlike anything he had ever seen before. In his world there were no such people. The closest he had ever seen was the villainess Lois Cipher. Back in the day she had been one of the big-league Arches, but her skin had been as red as Ming's robes. *Entirely different thing than this.*

"I am the *narrator*." The man annunciated the last word for clarity. "And you have arrived at the end of the story, it would appear." Cocking his head to one side, he evaluated them.

"So, now what?" Dave asked after several seconds of silence. "Do we choose between a blue pill and a red pill or something?"

Raising an eyebrow, the Narrator turned his ire towards the cameraman.

"Racist much? Really, why does every Casper-looking motherfucker always confuse me with Lawrence Fishburn? The man and I don't look anything alike." Dropping the formality, Mister Jackson's eyes flashed as he responded.

"Who's Casper?" Dave was truly at a loss. "And what's a *motherfucker*?"

While the others had been examining the narrator from a distance, Polly had crept around the perimeter, ever wary of the strange man who shouted at them now. Truly, his voice seemed to boom whenever he spoke. She was not sure what a *narrator* was, but she had her own suspicions. Cautiously she moved from cover to cover as she stayed alert.

"So what happens now?" Shrugging, Dave wondered what else there was to do in this place.

"Well, most likely you'll go in that empty space on the bookshelf over there. Then you'll sit there and gather dust for forty years until there is an estate sale, and then you'll be thrown into a trash bin and unceremoniously disposed of in a nearby landfill with the rest of the garbage." Careful to enunciate each word, the Narrator gestured to an empty space on one of the shelves. There appeared to be just enough room for one more book.

"I'm not following." Dave glanced between the narrator and the spot on the shelf.

"You, all of you," Gesturing to the four of them, the man with the ebony skin made it clear who he was referring to. "Are characters in a novel."

"Novel...?" Marv asked, his face screwed up in confusion. "You mean like a book?"

"Of course I mean *like a book*." Showing a surely attitude, the Narrator straightened his suit as he stood. "What else would the word mean?"

"I dunno." Marv shrugged. "I'm more of a magazine kinda guy."

Shoving his father aside, Dave approached the Narrator before asking the question that had been puzzling him.

"If we're characters in a book then what happens to us now?"

Shrugging, the dark man seemed indifferent. Gesturing to a paperback on the coffee table, he continued. "As I said earlier, you and your novel, really it's a novella, will be placed on that shelf where it will most likely never be read by anyone."

Scooping up the paperback, Dave began thumbing through the pages. As he read snippets here and there he was shocked to see that they were torn directly from his life. Flipping to the end, his jaw dropped open when he read about this very encounter with the Narrator.

"What the frack…?" Slamming the cover shut, the young cameraman's mind raced as he tried to put it all together. "How is this possible?"

"Do you mean; how is it possible that anyone actually buys this hack's books? That is a very good question, and one that I will be asking my soon-to-be former agent as soon as I get out of here. This gig is even worse than shilling for a credit card." Turning to face the audience, the Narrator's face switched to a smile. "What's in your wallet, motherfucker?"

"So what happens to us?" Marv wondered aloud.

"Like I said, you four will spend all eternity trapped in a novella written by a D-list writer. If you're lucky, you'll be eaten by termites or chewed up by a dog, thereby sparing you of your fate." Shrugging, Mister Jackson seemed more intent on getting to his next gig than explaining their destiny.

Believing that his master plan had been revealed, Polly had heard enough. Charging her weapons, she stepped out from behind Marv, a defiant look on her face.

"Die black demon!" Her shout echoed off the walls as both hands came up into tactical

stance. Without warning she fired her disruptor cannons at full power. Immediately the bright beam of energy shot out from her wrists, disintegrating the legendary actor in a flash of dust.

Dave shoved her angrily. "What the hell'd you do that for?"

"He just said that he was planning on imprisoning us in a book on that shelf. I thought he was that guy from Myst. Did you want me to wait until we were already trapped inside?" Incredulous, she could not understand their rebuke. "Besides, **you** killed God."

"It wasn't really God!" Dave waved that off. "Seriously, could you have at least waited until we asked a few more questions? Now the whole place smells like fried narrator."

"Yeah." Marvelous agreed. "I woulda liked to ask him how the hell we get out of here. I mean, you could die from boredom in a library. There's absolutely nothing to do here."

"Except read." Ming pointed out with a hint of irritation to his voice. Plucking a copy of *Calizona* off the shelf, he immediately smiled. "*Oooh*, this looks good."

"There's always the door." Dave pointed to the wooden portal across the room. It looked odd with the narrator-shaped scorch marks burnt into the plaster wall.

"What exactly is a thespian?" Wanda asked as she cautiously stepped over the floating letters.

"I think it's another word for a mime. Y'know, those people down at the park who pretend like they're in an invisible box." Dave showed a distasteful face as he thought of them.

"Hey, maybe it's a bathroom." Marv flashed a smile and started towards the door. "I been dying to drain the main vein. I practically peed my super suit when I smacked down here."

"Thank you for sharing, Dad." Polly shook her head dismissively.

Moving as a unit, Dave opened the door and they all peered in.

It was a messy little room, with bookshelves overflowing and cluttered shelves. The smell of burnt coffee and cigars seemed to permeate the office.

Sitting with his back to them was a man typing on a computer. Hidden by the office chair he sat in, they could only see his hands *klackety-klacking* away on the keys. Finally after several seconds he half turned to yell over his shoulder.

"I'm working! Get the fuck out, and don't let that damned cat in either. Fricking thing bugs me to get in, then as soon as I let it in, the damned thing wants out again."

He turned back to his work for a moment before stopping. Realizing that they were still standing there with the door open, he finally spun the chair around to face them.

"Oh, it's you." He said with a dour grumble.

Their initial reaction was to recoil at the sight of the man. Bald head, and a malformed face, he was unlike anyone in their galaxy; *he was ugly!* There was simply no other way to describe the man; he was quite distinctly and noticeably the ugliest human being they had ever seen. Even worse than the evil-eyed narrator they had just defeated.

Holding up a hand tentatively, Polly seemed almost as if she were going to touch his face as she looked at him curiously.

"Does it hurt?" She gestured to his face.

"Huh?" The man made an angry expression. "Listen to you; the crazy bitch who killed Samuel L. Jackson. Who does that? Every motherfucker on the fucking planet loves Samuel L. Jackson; you killed a national treasure. That's like kicking a black puppy; not only are you a racist, but you're an asshole too."

"But he was a black demon...?" She defended herself, though it was clear she was beginning to question her actions now.

"Ahhh, I see." The man in the chair seemed to make a connection. "You've never seen a black guy because in the 1930s universe of Flash Gordon and Buck Rogers, there were no minorities. Hell, even Ming was played by a white guy. I guess I shoulda thought about that before I put you in a room with Sam. Now there's no way he'll do the part, and I'll have to use Lawrence Fishburn."

"Who are you?" Dave asked, not interested in what happened in the last room.

"Me?" The man in the chair laughed openly. "I'm the writer. I'm the schmuck who wrote this steaming pile of shit you call a world."

"Then you claim to be God?" Dave asked, sure that it was all another faux reality.

"**Your** god maybe, but not THE god." Waving a hand as he spoke, he gestured to them before continuing. "I created all of you, and my Momma created me, and God created her. Does that fill in enough of the blanks for ya?"

Feeling skeptical after a series of tricks, Dave was clearly not convinced. He could still taste alien guts in his mouth from earlier, and that had all turned out to be complete fraud.

"Prove it." Folding his arms, Dave stood his ground.

"Mmmmkay." The ugly man in the chair agreed with a flippant smile. Spinning around, he began narrating as he typed. "All of a sudden, Captain Marvelous found himself wearing a pink tutu and tights."

Spinning back around, the writer was just in time to see Marv's super-suit replaced by an outfit that looked like it came from a little girl. A little snug in the crotch, the outfit left nothing to the imagination.

"It must have been cold in the pool, eh?" Looking over at Marv's crotch, he remarked with a cruel laugh.

"I'm a grower not a show-er." Mister Marvelous clasped his hand over his junk as his face turned red.

"Oh, better yet!" Again the writer spun about before narrating his own typing. "And Polly's clothes were suddenly transformed into a bikini that was on the verge of a wardrobe failure."

Gasping, the journalist was shocked when her already skimpy outfit was replaced with an itty-bitty, yellow, polka-dot bikini that **groaned** under the stress of her amble bosoms.

"Now that's good writing!" Leering as he pointed to the heroine, the writer seemed truly pleased with himself. "I'm just gonna take a few mental pictures, if that's okay with everyone…"

"The demon--*er*—narrator…" Dave corrected himself, "He said we were in a book…?"

"You are; you're characters in a pulp-fiction book set in the black & white era of cinema. Really, you're a homogenization of everything I've ever read or watched. You remember those movies the alien had? I stole lines or concepts from every one of 'em."

The four characters mulled this over before Dave finally spoke up.

"Nah. You're full of shit!"

The writer laughed openly at that. "You are not wrong about that, but the fact remains; you are just fictional characters in another one of my books. That's why she looks like Christina Hendricks, and Marvelous looks like Bruce Campbell, and Ming over there looks like Charles Middleton from the original movies, but talks like Stuey from *Family Guy*. It's something I like to do when I create characters; I model them on real people or the movie stars I want to play them. It helps create better characters."

"*They* all look like...*movie stars?*" Dave could tell by the context that this was an exalted thing. "What star do I look like?"

"Well that's just it." The writer stood up where he could look Dave over closely. "You don't look like anyone I know. You don't look like any movie stars, you don't look like that asshole at the bank today. You're just this fucking anomaly."

"Excuse?" Dave was offended.

"Don't give me that bullshit. You're a damned anomaly. You weren't even supposed to be a real character; I was gonna kill the cameraman every scene so Polly got someone new, over and over. It was gonna be the running gag of the story, how she just keeps calling 'em all Dave just because it's more convenient. But then I forgot to kill you in that first scene, and the next thing I know you're a regular cast member…then before I know it, you have super powers, and your father is secretly Darth Vader?"

"What…? No." Dave was not sure who that was.

Waving him off, the author walked around the cameraman as if examining him. "And now you've managed to stick around longer than Shaharizad. You were supposed to get killed every episode like Kenny from *SouthPark*. You were never supposed to be anything more than a plot device. This is what happens when I *pants* a book. I gotta go back to outlining."

Turning to leer at Polly, the Writer seemed to find her revulsion fascinating. Staring down at her bosoms that seemed to defy gravity, he gave a smirk.

"Y'know, as much as I like seeing you in that bikini, sooner or later you're gonna put out an eye with one of those things." Pretending to type on an invisible keyboard, he once again narrated his own text. "And in a flash, Polly's bikini was changed into one of Joan Harris's outfits. The red one with the little bow in the back."

The words had only just left his mouth when Polly gasped at the sensation of clothes growing to cover her body. Standing there in a shapely red dress, she felt an odd consciousness about it all. "This feels really familiar somehow…"

Turning away, the Writer stopped to admire Ming's flashy outfit. "And you my friend, you were from my mother's era. You were the villain who inspired George Lucas to create *Star Wars*. So essentially it was your stuff that inspired the guy who inspired me…and I created you…again. So basically you're literary refried beans."

"Did you hear that?" Elbowing Polly, Ming practically beamed. "I inspired him, indirectly, to create us. That was *alllll* me."

"He also called you refried beans." Polly pointed out before going back to admiring her outfit.

Standing alone, Dave had been trying to put the pieces together. Something troubled him about it all.

"If we are characters in a book, then we really are destined to be imprisoned for all eternity on a shelf, aren't we?"

Stopping to give him the evil eye, the Writer seemed irritated at this.

"*Hmmmph*; there you go, whining about your fate. You were supposed to be crewman number six in every scene, but instead you got to be the hero of the story. *Waaahhh*."

Dave stepped back surprised. "Isn't the story about me?"

"Oh listen to you, Tina Louise. No, *Gilligan's Island* is not about you. Did you not see the cover of this book? What's it say up there at the top? Eh? The book was supposed to be about that crimson dildo over there." Pointing, the Writer made it clear that Ming was the intended protagonist of the book. "Not only that, but I like to think that my books stay pretty active at the library, they don't just sit there gathering dust, they get checked out…a lot!"

There was a shuffling from the four as they seemed to doubt his writing skills.

"I dunno," Marv admitted sheepishly. "You created *us*."

"I do feel awfully derivative." Polly admitted as she looked over her dress. "But *damn* do I look good."

"Okay, looksee here." The author nodded as he regrouped. "I'll meet you all halfway. Now, you've all heard of Netflix, right?"

"Oh yes." There was agreement among the Supers. "We pray that if we are champions, one day we will go to Netflix heaven."

Raising his eyebrows skeptically, Ming added his own two cents. "I always pray to go to Showtime heaven."

"Weirdo." The Writer scowled at the man in red. "Anyhow, here's the deal I'll make with you guys, and gals; you all go back out there and give it your best fight, be the best champions and villains you know how to be, and I will do everything I can to sell this book to Netflix or HBO or one of those streaming services, and then you'll live forever in Streaming Heaven."

There was an *ooohing* sound from Mister Marvelous as he imagined himself in perpetual syndication. Just thinking about it made his ego swell.

Although it sounded like a lot, Polly had a concern with a major detail.

"But this can't be it, the end of the story. I'm still young, I don't want to end here. I want more life, more adventures…"

"*Well*, lemme show you something." Putting an arm around her, the Writer herded her over to his computer. Clicking on the screen with a handheld device, he pulled up a picture of a naked woman strapped to a bed. Beside her was a midget holding a bucket of grease.

"Doh!" He said before hastily closing the browser. "I was just…researching…*yeah, that's the ticket, I was researching.*" He lied, badly.

Finally pulling up the right window he showed them something.

"See, these are what's known as sequels. What happens is; if a story is popular, then there is a sequel, and another, and another, and sometimes they just keep going for generations, like *Star Trek*, or *Star Wars*…"

"Movie stars, star wars, BattleStar…" Ming shook his head disapprovingly. "Everything is stars with you people. You do realize that stars are nothing but big balls of hot gas?"

"That pretty much sums up most of our stars too." The Writer agreed with a frown. "But like I was saying, if we can make this first story good enough then there will be lots of sequels, and you'll get to go on all kinds of exciting adventures."

"Performing like your monkeys..." Polly seemed less than thrilled at the prospect.

"Girl, you get to fly around the galaxy in space ships, shooting lasers and death rays, wearing a leather bikini...*and you're complaining*. I would quit my day job in a heartbeat to do your job! I mean, what more could you ask for? Your job is kick ass, and it's not like real people get killed when you fuck up. They're just words, that's all. No actual animals are ever harmed in the making of my books. True fact." Flopping down into his chair again, the Writer seemed pleased with himself.

"I want more lines." Wanda's request sparked little surprise in the room. "And my wardrobe designer from *Mad Men*. No one knew how to dress me like Janie did."

"Done and done, and agreed; Janie Bryant shoulda got a fucking Nobel Prize for your wardrobe in *Mad Men*." The writer's eyes had not risen higher than her chest as he seemed captivated by her red dress.

"I want a little more character development." Dave was nonplussed. "And could I get beat up less, please."

"Not gonna happen. Your only real power is rope-a-dope, so you just gotta do the Rocky thing, and defeat them by using your head to punch their fists until they are too tired to fight anymore." Laughing, the Writer seemed to find glee in tormenting the cameraman.

"I want a new love interest, maybe an Andorian woman." Marv looked like he was still mulling over the choices in his mind. "Now that I can see colors, I'd like to check out one of the green ones. Is that Zoe Zaldana chick available? I really respect her body…of work." He added the last part as Polly shot him a look.

"As long as we are giving Santa our Christmas lists," Ming slid into the conversation. "Is there any way I could get one of those giant-head screens like the Wizard had in Oz? That was really quite dope, as my minions would say."

Half a smile on his face, the Writer finally gave a nod.

"So that's it. The book is finished, Professor Zero is vanquished. I'm gonna get a fresh cup of coffee, maybe beat-off to some Christina Hendricks clipart, then go back and edit this fucking mess of a manuscript. And while I'm doing that I need each and every one of you characters to get back out there and give it your all. Go out on that stage and break a leg…not your own, but definitely break some bones. You do your part, and I'll do my part, and let's see if we can't sell some books and maybe even a screenplay."

Turning back to his keyboard, the Writer ignored them as he resumed work. One by one they each shuffled out the door of the cramped little office until only Marv remained. After a long silence, punctuated by the Writer's keystrokes, the author finally turned to him.

"What?" He asked the Super.

"While you're doing that editing stuff, could you…maybe make me…a grower AND a show-*er*." Giving a sheepish shrug, Marvelous seemed sincere.

"Klaatu barada necktie!" The Writer waved his hand and made Marv vanish in a puff of smoke.

"There, I said your words…mostly." He laughed at his own joke like an asshole.

Still staring at the empty spot where the Super had been standing just a few seconds ago, the Writer could only shake his head sadly.

"That is the last time I drink Absinth and try to write a book. That shit really messes you up."

The end

If you enjoyed this novella, then please review it on Amazon.com.

Struggling Indie authors like Ralph desperately need your support. Every review helps more people find our books and stay in the writing business.

Glossary

Shaharizad The heroine of 1001 Arabian Nights. Set to be executed after her wedding night, she managed to outsmart the hangman by telling a new story every night for 1001 nights.

Tina Louise The starlet had been led to believe that she would be the star of Gilligan's Island.

Joan Harris A character in the TV show Mad Men, played by <u>Christina Hendricks</u>.

Klaatu barada necktie was the punch line of a joke in **Army of Darkness**, starring <u>Bruce Campbell</u>. The phrase was a humorous mispronunciation of the phrase **Klaatu barada nikto** that originated in the classic 1951 movie **The Day the Earth Stood Still**.

Ming's ship is named the *Mors Machina* which is Latin for Death Machine

Nati interfectorem is Latin for Natural Born Killer

Magna Turci is Latin for Big Turd

Culus Capitus is Latin for Asshole Head

Ming's personal ship, the ***Sexus Navis*** is Latin for **Sex Ship**.

Yes, I got tired of making up names and just used Google translator to come up with names. So sue me.

Part of my writing process for building characters is to have a real person or actor in mind when I write them. For this book these <u>are the people I envisioned:</u>

Mister Marvelous...*Bruce Campbell*
Polly/Wanda...*Christina Hendricks*
Ming voiced by *Stuey from Family Guy*
Anybody could play Dave.
Samuel L Jackson...*Lawrence Fishburn*
[just kidding, Sam!]
God...*Patrick Stewart*
Alien...*Groot*
Professor Zero...*Eddie Izzard*
StarFire...*Charlize Theron*
Lotus...*Tom Hiddleston*
The Manganeese were all Belters
Captain Legend...*Zapp Brannigan*